ST. MARY PARISH LIBRARY
3 3446 00835 2
S0-HIN-864

LP
PAT
Patten, Lewis B. author.
Five rode west
FRA
9-19

ST. MARY PARISH LIBRARY
FRANKLIN, LOUISIANA

Five Rode West

Center Point
Large Print

Also by Lewis B. Patten and available from Center Point Large Print:

Shadow of the Gun
Cañon Creek
Gun This Man Down
Hang Him High
The Cheyenne Pool
Lone Rider

This Large Print Book carries the Seal of Approval of N.A.V.H.

LEWIS B. PATTEN

Five Rode West

CENTER POINT LARGE PRINT
THORNDIKE, MAINE

This Center Point Large Print edition
is published in the year 2019 by arrangement with
Golden West Literary Agency.

Copyright © 1958 by Lewis B. Patten.
Copyright © 1966 by Lewis B. Patten in the British
Commonwealth. Copyright © renewed 1986 by
Catherine C. Patten.

All rights reserved.

Originally published in the US by
Fawcett Publications, Inc.
Originally published in the UK by Jenkins.

The text of this Large Print edition is unabridged.
In other aspects, this book may vary
from the original edition.
Printed in the United States of America
on permanent paper.
Set in 16-point Times New Roman type.

ISBN: 978-1-64358-272-6 (hardcover)
ISBN: 978-1-64358-276-4 (paperback)

Library of Congress Cataloging-in-Publication Data

Names: Patten, Lewis B., author.
Title: Five rode west / Lewis B. Patten.
Description: Large Print edition. | Thorndike, Maine :
Center Point Large Print, 2018. | "Originally published in the US by
Fawcett Publications, Inc. Originally published in the UK by Jenkins."
Identifiers: LCCN 2019017869| ISBN 9781643582726 (hardcover :
alk. paper) | ISBN 9781643582764 (pbk. : alk. paper)
Subjects: LCSH: Large type books. | GSAFD: Western stories.
Classification: LCC PS3566.A79 F58 2018 | DDC 813/.54—dc23
LC record available at https://lccn.loc.gov/2019017869

Five Rode West

CHAPTER 1

THERE were three of them. They rode through the dappled afternoon shade of aspens and scattered spruce high on the side of the mountain so that there would be no one in the valley below to say they had passed and to give their descriptions. They were headed west.

Clyde Valle rode in the lead, slouching in his weathered saddle. Behind him came Rufe Thebus, frowning slightly as his confused and forgetful mind tried to understand why he was here and what they were doing. Behind Rufe came Johnny Sauls, who was just a kid of fifteen trying not to show his fright.

Ahead, the country became wilder, rising ridge after ridge until it reached the haze-shrouded slopes of the monstrous mesa twenty-five miles away. The land ahead appeared to the three like a flight of steps which they had to climb before reaching the easier going of the mesa top. The sides of those western ridges, and of the mesa itself, were spotted with golden groves of quakies, but their over-all color was the deep, gray-green of spruce.

To the left of the trio lay a wide valley,

dotted with brown stacks of wild hay and criss-crossed with fences. In the center of the valley a road wound along and stretched away into the rearward distance like a tan ribbon. Occasionally Clyde saw a wagon on it, or a horseman, and once, near noon, he had seen a stagecoach dusting busily along.

A silent trio was this, each occupied with his own private thoughts. Oddly enough, there seemed no particular enthusiasm in any of them for the thing they were going to do. Rather, their faces showed grim determination and perhaps a hint of doubt. They were out to collect one debt—and to pay another—in the only way they could. And while the method of collection was illegal, none of them seemed concerned with its illegality. Committed to their course, they now were concerned only with avoiding detection.

Clyde, leading, was a tall man crowding thirty. His face was faintly hollow-cheeked, and very dark from the sun. It was covered with a soft stubble of tawny whiskers.

His nose was straight and generous above a mouth that might have seemed soft in a softer face. That quality was lost, however, in the over-all harshness of his features, and in the bitterness that lurked behind his dark brown eyes.

His chin was a jutting outcropping of strength. Altogether, his was a good face, and one most men would have been inclined to trust on sight.

Clyde was lean, his belly flat and hard-muscled. From the waist, he tapered out and up to a pair of wide and muscled shoulders. His hair was tawny as his beard and worn so long that it almost completely covered his neck.

From time to time during the long day he had glanced behind, ostensibly to speak to his companions. Actually, he was scanning their back trail, seeking another glimpse of the solitary rider he had first seen early in the morning. He didn't want to alarm the others; so he said nothing to them about it.

The sun sank slowly behind the mesa ahead, and stained the scattered clouds a brilliant salmon pink. The three dropped into a ravine that was dark and cool with shadow. They halted in a grove of willows near the narrow tumbling stream in its bottom.

Half a dozen deer broke from the willows and bounded stiff-legged up the far slope. Clyde dismounted and yanked his ancient Spencer from the saddle boot. Kneeling, he followed the leading deer with the gun for a moment and then fired. The buck dropped, kicked a few times and then lay still. The others went over the top of the ridge, briefly skylined against the brilliant clouds before they disappeared.

Clyde slipped the rifle back into the boot and mounted again. He said, "Gather up some wood. We're having steaks for supper."

He rode up the slope and dismounted beside the deer. Quickly he opened its belly and cleaned it out. He cut off its head and feet and made a hole in its flank large enough to slip over the saddle horn. He hoisted it to his saddle, secured it on the horn, then mounted behind it. He rode down the slope at a walk, feeling the heat of the deer carcass under his legs. It was now almost dark.

He hung the deer in a tree and skinned it carefully. Rufe Thebus had a fire going. Clyde went to the stream and washed the blood from his hands. He returned, drying them on the legs of his pants. He squatted beside the fire and spread his hands toward it, saying, "We'd better wait until it cools a little. A man can get sick eating meat before the heat goes out of it."

Rufe looked at him, the familiar blankness in his eyes. Clyde had known Rufe all his life. He liked the older man. It wasn't Rufe's fault that a Yankee rifle bullet had addled his mind. When this was over, at least Rufe would have enough money to live comfortably until he died. He wouldn't have to take any more abuse from the hangers-on in Viereck's saloon, where he worked as a swamper.

Rufe was an inch shorter than Clyde, but he weighed about the same. He had a sharp nose that seemed to be pointing to the cropped beard below it. His vague eyes were circled by tiny wrinkles like crow's feet. His mind might be vague, but Clyde doubted if that would impair his efficiency as a fighter. Maybe he couldn't think for himself, but he didn't know what fear was, and he'd do as he was told.

The present blankness in Rufe's eyes made Clyde realize that Rufe had forgotten why they were here and what they were going to do.

Rufe licked his lips and cleared his throat. He looked at Johnny Sauls and then back at Clyde. He said, "Clyde, what are we doing here? I ought to be down at the saloon. . . ."

Clyde said patiently, "You quit your job, Rufe. You don't have to go back any more."

Rufe frowned, trying to drag from his mind something he couldn't quite reach. Clyde said, "We're going into the Ute Reservation, Rufe. We're going after a herd of cattle. Remember?"

Rufe nodded, smiling uncertainly. But the frown remained on his brow. Clyde said, "They're government cattle, Rufe. The Utes are in revolt and the Yankee Army is trying to put it down. Over a hundred men under a Major Thornburg left Fort Steele several days ago. But the Indians jumped them fifteen or twenty miles north of White River and pinned them down."

Johnny Sauls burst out, with the intolerance of youth, "Oh Christ! Do we have to go all over that again?"

Clyde said, "Shut up, Johnny. We've got to

get it fixed in Rufe's mind before we get there. Otherwise, he's liable to forget. No telling what he might do if he does."

He returned his glance to Rufe. "Think, Rufe. Those cattle belong to the government. We're going to take them. The Indians don't want them; they'd rather eat venison. And the Army's too busy to be worrying about cattle. So it's made to order. We ride in and push the cattle out. We drive them into Utah and re-brand. Then we sell them."

Rufe's frown disappeared. He remembered now, Clyde saw. Rufe grinned, pleased with himself. "I remember now. We're collecting something on what the Yankees took from us all in Georgia, ain't we? We're doing this because Carrie wants us to."

Clyde nodded. "That's right, Rufe. We're doing it for Carrie."

He got up and went to where the deer carcass was hanging. He cut out part of the backstrap, laid it on a rock and sliced it. He got a skillet from behind his saddle and greased it with tallow cut from the deer's rump. He put it on the fire and when it was smoking, dropped in the steaks.

Covertly he watched Johnny Sauls. Johnny started at each small noise. He kept glancing around into the wall of darkness beyond the fire.

Clyde went back down to the creek, the savory odor of frying meat in his nostrils. He squatted and splashed water into his face and over his head.

He scrubbed vigorously, then got up, running his fingers through his hair. He unsaddled his horse, picketed him out, then returned to the fire. Worry plagued his mind as he remembered that solitary horseman he'd seen this morning on their trail.

The steaks were done. The three ate with their fingers and sipped scalding coffee from tin cups. Afterward, Rufe took the cups and skillet to the stream and scoured them out with sand.

Clyde noticed that Johnny Sauls stayed either close to the fire or close to Clyde himself. The kid's eyes were scared and he was jumpy as hell. If he was this way now, how would it be later, in Indian country?

Clyde shook his head, suddenly doubting his ability to carry this off. Three men just weren't enough. And Clyde didn't even have three.

He only had Rufe, addle-witted and unable to think for himself, and Johnny Sauls, who was already scared enough to jump out of his skin.

The fire died to a bed of coals. Clyde got his rifle and blanket and went out into the darkness beyond the fire. He splashed across the creek and climbed the slope beyond for about fifty feet. Rufe and Johnny bedded down right beside the fire.

Clyde hollowed a small depression for himself in the ground, digging with the sharp edge of a flat rock. Then he rolled up in his blanket and lay down.

He stared up at the stars without really seeing

them, for suddenly his mind was full of the past, of things that had happened so long ago back home in Georgia, of the things that had led him directly to this.

He'd been ten when the war began, and it had somehow not been real to him at first. It had been pageantry and excitement, men standing around arguing States Rights and Slavery and about a place called Fort Sumter. Then Clyde's father had gone away to fight, leaving the place for his mother and grandfather and himself to run.

Clyde thought he knew the reality of war when the news came that his father had been killed. His grandfather, angered beyond endurance, tried to join up, but they wouldn't have him. He came home with a furious face that somehow never again lost either its bitterness or its brooding fury.

And his mother's grief was unending.

But Clyde had not yet seen the reality of war. He had only touched its edges.

Staring up at the starlit sky, Clyde's eyes became bright. His forehead glistened with sweat. The past became reality in his mind as he lived it, saw it all again as though no span of years lay between it and the present.

First had come the long lines of ragged, bloody, exhausted men in gray. They passed for days, dispirited, defeated. Then came the sound of cannon, distant at first, but growing ever nearer, as the days and hours passed. Then the rattle of musket fire in the woods. The battle raged in the fields, in the woods, in the yard itself. But the tide moved on as Sherman's army ground along relentlessly toward the sea.

In the wake of that tide came another army, of despoilers, of looters, of deserters. Clyde saw his birthright, the house, the slave quarters—all of it put to the torch. He saw the crops wantonly destroyed by sections of rail dragged across the land.

He saw his mother struck brutally to the ground, and his grandfather shot because he dared protest and back up his protest with an ancient musket.

With an effort, he forced his mind out of the past to the solitary rider he had seen following them this morning. It wasn't fear that troubled him, but not knowing—uneasiness at his inability to guess who followed them, and why.

He couldn't have anyone know where they were going or what they intended to do. Only the need for secrecy had made him try to do a ten-man job with so small and uncertain a group. Rufe Thebus and Johnny Sauls were scarcely the men he would have chosen for this.

He tried to sleep, but his nerves were strung too tight. The responsibility was entirely on him. He must have a plan.

The wide valley of White River lay about seventy miles to the west. He knew how to get there, but otherwise was completely unfamiliar with the country. Most white men were. It was Ute reservation and neither the Utes nor the government looked favorably upon trespassers.

All Clyde knew, all he cared about, was that there were a thousand or more fat white-faced cattle in the White River Valley—cattle about which nobody cared at the moment.

All summer rumors had flown thick and fast—rumors of a ranch attacked here, a town burned there. Some of the rumors had been true, some false. But because of the rumors this plan had been born. The Utes were getting ready for an uprising before the winter set in. And when they did, the cattle would be left unguarded.

And the uprising had come. Rumor had it that they'd massacred everybody but the women at the White River Indian Agency. Rumor had it that troops, summoned by the Agent, had left Fort Steele and had been attacked somewhere north of the Agency.

Upon the truth of these rumors lay the chance Clyde had of accomplishing what he had set out to do. If the Indians were engaging the troops and if the battle lasted long enough, the White River Valley would be open, free of whites, comparatively free of Indians as well. With a little luck, Clyde and his companions could ride through fast, gathering their cattle, and be gone before anyone was wiser.

They'd drive west into Utah and halt in some

hidden canyon while they changed the brands and while the new brands healed.

Clyde smiled grimly in the darkness. That was the best of it. That was the way it would be if everything went smoothly. But everything wouldn't go smoothly. It never did. And in his case there were too many imponderables, too many unknowns.

He tried not to think of what the worst would be, but he couldn't help himself. Suppose they found the White River swarming with hostiles? Suppose the troops were in control?

Suppose, too, that he lost either Johnny or Rufe? He'd have to turn back, because the job couldn't possibly be done with less than three. One had to ride each valley slope, and one was needed on the valley floor to hold the cattle already gathered and to keep them moving west.

Angrily, Clyde shook himself and burrowed deeper into his blankets. A chill flowed down the slope off the ridge and he began to shiver. He considered going down by the fire, but discarded the idea almost at once. There was still that unknown rider on their trail.

His jaw hardened. Tomorrow evening their direction would be established. Tomorrow evening, if the man were still on their trail, Clyde was going to find out who he was and what he wanted. And have it out with him.

Sleep came at last. He woke several times

during the night—to listen intently for the sound that had disturbed him. Each time it proved to be some prowling animal.

He woke in the first chill of dawn. He was numb with cold. He got up and stamped his feet and beat his body with his arms, trying to restore circulation. His breath made great clouds of steam in the frosty air.

A bunch of deer bounded up the far ridge and started over the top, but they changed course abruptly on top of the ridge and instead of crossing over, veered back at right angles to Clyde and eventually disappeared. Clyde's eyes narrowed. The deer had seen something on the other side of the ridge, something that had turned them aside.

It could be a coyote or wolf, or even a bear, but Clyde didn't think it was. No. It was a man who had turned the deer, the man who had been on their trail.

He walked downslope toward their camp, still chilled and shivering. He stopped at the creek and splashed a little icy water into his face.

Rufe was already up, building a fire. Johnny was shivering visibly in his blankets, awake but reluctant to get up. Clyde stirred him gently with the toe of his foot. "Get up, kid. You going to sleep all day?"

Johnny grunted with protest, but he got up,

shivering and rubbing his eyes. Clyde flung a glance up the ridge along the way they had come yesterday, but he saw nothing.

He knew he could go up there now and discover once and for all who it was on their trail. But he didn't, deciding instead to wait until tonight. They'd be up on top of that high plateau by nightfall. And once up there, their direction would be unmistakable. Also unmistakable would be the pursuer's intent, if he was on their trail.

Clyde went and squatted beside the fire, spreading his stiff hands toward its welcome heat. Smoke drifted into his face. He squinted against it, frowning.

When he had warmed a little, he went to the deer carcass and cut another section of loin from its back. He sliced it and carried it to Rufe to cook. Then he returned and wrapped the chilled carcass with his blanket to keep the flies from it. He cut it down and laid it beside his saddle.

Returning to the fire, he studied Johnny's glum, unsmiling face. Johnny's life had been tied in with his own until Johnny seemed almost like a brother to him. Johnny, a baby then, had been picked up by Carrie Quaintance on the way west from Georgia. Hearing him crying out in the woods, she'd left Clyde and Rufe and Lacy, and had searched until she found him. They'd looked around afterward for his kin, but there wasn't a soul within a mile. So Carrie had kept him and carried him west with her into the territories. She'd named him Johnny Sauls after an uncle of hers who had died in the war.

When the steaks were done and the coffee boiled, they ate. By the time they had finished and had saddled their horses, the sun was touching the high rim of the mesa ahead.

Clyde slung the wrapped deer carcass over the rump of his horse and tied it down. They could eat it fresh until they got close to the Ute Reservation. But unless they wanted to eat it raw, they'd have to cook it with their last fire before entering the reservation.

He rode out, leading, and at the top of the ridge looked back. He saw nothing.

The sun felt good against his back, and gradually the night's chill thawed from his bones. He glanced at the sky to the north, and was immeasurably relieved to find it clear.

This was late September, and it could storm any day now, particularly here in the high country. He hoped it wouldn't, though. This job would be hard enough without having to fight a blizzard.

Yet even the sun could not wholly lighten Clyde's spirits. A feeling of dread and foreboding was on him this morning, a feeling that told him this job would not go well. He knew suddenly that he should give it up. But he didn't stop his horse and he didn't turn aside. His face grim, he rode toward the west.

CHAPTER 2

RIDGE by ridge, the land dropped behind, and the three riders drew gradually closer to the high slope of the monstrous mesa ahead. The valley that had lain to their left pinched down until it became a canyon, and gradually disappeared altogether in the rising terrain.

Clyde glanced behind occasionally, and once saw the dark speck of the pursuing rider in the distance. The man was still with them, then, and it could be no accident that he was. Certainty of this drew Clyde's nerves tight and put a frown of worried concentration between his eyes.

Trying to forget the man and the problem he presented until the time came to do something about him, Clyde turned his mind again to the past, remembering.

Strange how a man's early experiences put their indelible mark on his later life. It was this way with Clyde, and he supposed with everyone else to one degree or another.

He and his mother had buried Clyde's grandfather in the family burial plot not far from the smoldering ruins of the house. Then, hungry and unutterably weary, they had started out for the Quaintance place, three miles away.

Clyde's mother died on the way. And Clyde went on to the Quaintance place, scarcely conscious in his terrible feeling of loss.

Carrie herself, then eighteen, had come back with him, carrying lantern and shovel. They buried Clyde's mother there in the woods. Afterward they dragged themselves back to the Quaintance house, which also smoldered in blackened ruins.

A fire burned in the middle of the great, spacious lawn. A pot of greens and ham shanks hung over the fire. Carrie ladled out a plateful for Clyde and brought it to him where he sat exhausted on the ground.

He looked up at her dumbly, too filled with grief to eat, too tired to move.

Carrie Quaintance was no stranger to Clyde, but, being older, she had always been beyond his reach. That hadn't stopped him from loving her with an adolescent fervor that almost amounted to worship. He could remember walking all the way here on many occasions just on the chance that he'd see her—either riding her spirited mare wildly across the fields, jumping fences with laughing recklessness, or walking quietly across the lawn in a frivolous, billowing gown of silk.

He remembered the excitement that clutched

his throat when he was near her, and her delicate perfume was a heady drug in his nostrils.

She was different now. Her hair was uncombed, hanging angled around her smudged face. Her dress was torn in several places, covered with soot, and mud, and spilled food. But Clyde loved her only the more because somehow she seemed less unattainable than she had before.

With them around the fire were Rufe Thebus, a bloody bandage around his head and a vacant look in his eyes, and Lacy, Carrie's eight-year-old sister, whose face was tear-streaked and white with terror. Rufe was the son of the Quaintance overseer, who had been invalided out of his unit and had made his way home.

For a long while, Clyde's eyes dumbly worshipped Carrie, but at last they closed and he slept. At midnight, Carrie woke him, putting a roughened hand over his mouth so he would not cry out. "Get up, Clyde. We're leaving."

"Why? Where are we going?"

"Away. West, I suppose. Anywhere where people are still human and not animals like they've become here."

Frightened as he was, he did not protest. And so, the four set out by night, walking across the endless miles.

Carrie stole, and begged, and, he realized now, sometimes even sold herself to get enough food to keep them alive. In her eyes, which had always been so soft, a hardness grew, a hate that afterward never quite died away.

And they found young Johnny Sauls, less than a year old, weakened by hunger and sickness. He would have died but for an old Negro couple that sheltered the party in their tiny cabin until he had recovered enough to be taken along.

Days grew into weeks, and weeks into months. Clyde matured swiftly during those months of hardship. He grew wiry and tough. He learned to forage and to steal. And his worship of Carrie, who held the party together as though life itself depended upon her doing so, grew until it was for him the beginning and end of everything.

West from the ravaged fields of Georgia they traveled, west toward the territories. Time ceased to have meaning. They lived like animals, shunning human contacts. Rufe's head wound healed but his mind did not. Carrie and Clyde and Lacy grew hard and tough and strong. They would never now be taken for the gently reared Southern aristocrats they had been. The baby Johnny Sauls, having survived his early crisis, lived and grew amazingly.

Eventually they reached Colorado and there they stopped. But they did not prosper. Indeed, they barely existed. This was a land peopled by Yankees, whom they all had grown to hate with an intensity nearly equaling that of Carrie

Quaintance, who determinedly kept their hate alive.

Rufe was fit to hold only certain menial jobs. And Clyde went to school, along with Lacy. Later, Johnny started school and Clyde went to work.

Perhaps, Clyde realized now, all that had made it bearable for Carrie was her dream that someday, somewhere, an opportunity for revenge would present itself. And this—these fat cattle waiting in the Ute Reservation—had become that opportunity.

They reached the slope of the high mesa at noon, and halted. Clyde built a small fire and they cooked enough meat to last several meals, just in case. He carefully stowed what they did not use in his capacious saddlebags.

While the three allowed their horses to graze, Clyde stretched out on the sun-warmed ground and closed his eyes. Johnny Sauls sat down beside him and took out his pocket knife. He began to whittle nervously. After a while he asked, his voice a shade too casual, "What do the Utes do to a man if they catch him, Clyde, stake him out on an ant hill?"

"It's Apaches that do that, kid. Even then, they've got to hate a man considerable before they treat him that way. Besides the Utes won't catch us. Stop fretting about it."

"You think I'm scared, don't you?"

Clyde opened his eyes and grinned. "I know you are. You'd be a fool if you weren't."

"Are you scared?"

Clyde nodded. "There's no shame in being scared. It's natural, like yanking your hand away from a fire when you burn it. The thing is, not to let it get you, to go on and do what you have to do, scared or not."

"Rufe don't seem scared."

Clyde looked at Rufe, who was fiddling with his saddle. He shook his head. "No. Rufe isn't scared. He hasn't got enough of his wits left to think ahead. That's the only reason."

He thought of the man on their trail, and suddenly called, "Rufe, come here a minute."

Rufe abandoned his saddle and shuffled over. Clyde asked, "Did you ever talk about this down at the saloon, Rufe?"

"Talk about what, Clyde?"

"This trip we're taking."

Rufe looked at him. His eyes were more rational than they usually were.

Clyde said, "Think, Rufe."

Rufe shook his head. But he did not meet Clyde's eyes.

Clyde said, "I won't raise hell with you, Rufe. I just want to know. I know how they tormented you down there. You're sure you didn't say anything about being rich soon?"

Rufe looked up. There was shame in his eyes.

"Well, I did say somethin' about that, Clyde. One of 'em tripped me and I dumped a spittoon all over the floor. I'm sorry, Clyde."

"Never mind, Rufe." He got up, stretching. "Let's go."

Each of the three caught his own horse and saddled. Clyde mounted and led out.

The slope of the plateau stretched ahead in a steep and steady grade which was dotted with clumps of scrub oak, turning brown from the season's first early frosts. Higher, the pale yellow of quakies made a beautiful contrast against the deep blue of the sky and the darker green of the tall, brooding spruces and pines.

Sage chickens fluttered up in flocks from their path and grouse wings hammered a tattoo in the still air, startling no matter how many times you heard them.

Deer abounded on the slope, and once, Clyde saw a small herd of elk high above him on the grade.

Now, he saw the pursuer often, for they were now far above the surrounding terrain. But the distance was too great for recognition.

All afternoon they traveled. In mid-afternoon, they followed a game trail up through the shelf of rimrock that guarded the top. Clyde sent Rufe and Johnny ahead, while he dismounted and stood at the edge of the rim, staring back.

The pursuer had gained on them during the day.

Perhaps he was crowding his horse for fear of letting the trail go cold. In any event, he was now no more than four or five miles behind. Tonight, Clyde thought, they'd make camp early. Tonight he'd backtrack a couple of miles and take the man by surprise.

He went on, then, catching Rufe and Johnny before he had gone a mile. He didn't miss the way they looked at him as he rode up. It was a look of dependence and faith. It was the kind of look a father might get from his son.

Clyde felt a sudden twinge of guilt. What if he were leading them to their deaths? Again that odd foreboding possessed him.

Were they doing the right thing? Given a free choice, would Rufe think they were? Would Johnny? Or were they both doing this against their wills simply because they owed it to Carrie?

Clyde swung around in his saddle and looked at Johnny. The boy had been like a younger brother to him now for almost fifteen years. He asked, "Johnny, do you really want to do this? Or would you rather cut away and forget about it?"

Johnny's hair was yellow as a quakie leaf. On his smooth cheeks was a down of yellow fuzz. His eyes were blue and against his hair made much the same contrast that the quakie leaves made against the sky.

His eyes were a little puzzled as he looked at

Clyde. He said, “Carrie wants us to,” as though that were answer enough.

Clyde felt briefly shamed. And yet he knew, even if the others did not, how little chance they had of bringing it off, of coming through alive.

He looked at Johnny again. Johnny frowned slightly as he said, “Carrie’s been like a mother to me. She picked me up in the woods when I would have died. She wants us to do this, so we got to do it.”

Clyde turned away with an inward shrug. He thought of Carrie, of the way she had looked when she’d told him about this plan of hers.

It had been less than a week ago. Carrie had come in, radiant as a girl, her dark eyes sparkling and a smile on her lips. “Clyde, I got the most wonderful idea from something I saw in the paper today. It said that there are over a thousand cattle in the White River Valley near the Indian Agency.”

“What about them?”

She came and flung her arms around him and kissed him on the mouth. He tightened his arms around her and pulled her hungrily against him. He muttered, “Carrie, damn the cattle! I want you to marry me. We’ve waited too long now.”

“Clyde, can’t you see? This is what we’ve been dreaming about all these years. You and Rufe and Johnny can ride in there and take those cattle. You can drive them over into Utah and re-brand them. Then you can sell them. Clyde, do you know what a thousand cattle will bring? Over thirty thousand dollars!"

He shrugged. "*If* we can get them out."

"You can. I know you can. There are no white men in the valley. And there won't be any Indians, either. They're all up north fighting the soldiers from Fort Steele."

Clyde had been reluctant at first. Very reluctant. It seemed an impossible scheme. It was fraught with risk. Besides, Clyde had no particular desire to be rich.

But, looking into Carrie's face, happy and radiant for the first time in months, he found himself wavering. She had exulted, "When you've done that, Clyde, we'll be married. I promised. There'll be something to live for again. Oh, Clyde!"

And so he'd agreed. And had found his own enthusiasm mounting under the stimulus of Carrie's contagious excitement.

The issue of stealing from the government bothered him not at all. All he had to do was remember the war, and the wanton destruction which Sherman had left behind. No, this was not stealing. This was the simple collection of a debt.

Now, he thought of Carrie, of the way she looked, still slim as a girl, but with a woman's power to heat his blood. He let himself anticipate the delicious intimacy of being married to her.

He thought of what he owed to her—what all of them owed to her.

Firmly he put out of his mind a small, nagging doubt that hovered there.

The horses plodded along patiently, and Clyde didn't try to hurry. Time enough for that later. Let the horses save their strength for now.

The afternoon wore itself away in dreary silence. Rufe whistled tunelessly for a while, then stopped. And at last, near four o'clock, Clyde drew rein in a little, brushy ravine and swung from his horse.

Johnny started to gather twigs and sticks for a fire as soon as his horse was picketed out. Clyde said softly, "No fire yet, Johnny."

He tipped back his hat and looked at the boy. Johnny was almost as tall as he was himself, but there was no solidity to his body. He was stringy and bony and thin, much as Clyde had been at the end of the war.

His face was speckled with freckles, and his mouth, unfirmed by either years or experience, was inclined to quiver imperceptibly in times of stress. Johnny asked, "How come no fire? We ain't in Indian country yet, are we?"

"Nope. Somebody trailing us. I'll go back and have a look presently. Meantime, go on and gather wood if you want. We'll have a fire later."

He lay down in the grass and pulled his hat over his face to cover his eyes against the glare of the dying sun. He could hear Rufe and Johnny moving around, gathering a night's supply of wood. He could hear, after that, the sound of Johnny's knife as he whittled shavings with which to start the fire.

His mind was ticking off the time it would take their pursuer to come in close.

And he was worried. Who was the man? Was it someone who had heard Rufe talking in the saloon? And if it was, what did he want? A share of the proceeds, Clyde supposed. Well, he'd decide what to do when he found out who the man was and what he wanted.

He shrugged inwardly, and cautioned himself not to borrow trouble. There'd be enough of that later without borrowing it now.

The sun dropped steadily. After about half an hour, Clyde got up. He slid his .36 caliber Navy Colt's revolver out of its holster and absently checked loads and nippes. Then without glancing either at Johnny or Rufe, he stalked away, afoot.

The grass whispered beneath his feet as he walked. It was dry and brittle and dusty. A rabbit scurried away.

The mesa top, which from below had appeared to be flat, was not flat at all. Instead, it was like a rolling prairie, with ridges divided by long, shallow ravines, all pointing toward the rim. Clyde kept himself hidden by a low, rounded ridge that fingered in that direction.

After he had gone a quarter of a mile, he topped it cautiously and peered along the trail they had made today. The rider was close now, no more than a mile distant. He was riding head down, intent on the trail. Occasionally he would look up and glance ahead.

Clyde calculated the stranger's course, studied the topography of the land for a moment, and planned his interception.

A gully cut away from the top of this ridge, shallow here and hardly adequate to hide a man's crawling body. Farther down, though, close to where the stranger would cross it, it appeared to be nearly four feet deep.

Clyde dropped to his belly and crawled over the top of the ridge. Using brush as cover, he crawled to where the gully began. He was careful to move slowly and deliberately, so that no quick movements would attract the stranger's eye.

In about ten minutes, he reached the place he sought. Cautiously, he poked his head up to take a look.

The rider had followed the course which Clyde had figured he would. Clyde kept his head up only long enough to catch a fleeting glimpse and to be sure of this. Then ducked out of sight.

The gully was wider here, and flat-bottomed. Clyde crouched against the side nearest the pursuing rider and waited. His muscles tensed.

He heard the horse's hoofbeats drawing near. A kicked stone fell into the gulch, struck his arm and rolled away. A tiny avalanche of loose dirt preceded the horse into the gully.

Even as he moved, a chord of familiarity stirred in Clyde's mind. He came erect with a single, smooth movement, seized the rider's leg and yanked him from the saddle.

The rider gave a small shriek of surprise and alarm, and Clyde let go the leg as though it was hot, leaving the rider rolling in the bare sand of the gully's bottom.

The horse jumped and ran a dozen yards. Then he turned to look back at Clyde and his downed rider.

Clyde stared in disbelief. Then a grin began at the corners of his wide mouth. The grin grew into a laugh that was deep and hearty, tinged with relief.

The pursuer sat up on the ground. Her hat had fallen off. Now her hair cascaded in a black, gleaming tangle around her small, oval face. She said furiously, "Laugh, darn you." Her face was flushed with anger, but there was something else in her eyes, a kind of uneasiness.

Clyde stopped laughing. "What the hell do you think you're doing 'way out here?"

"Following you." Lacy's chin came up. "You're not going to send me back, either."

"The hell I'm not. This is no job for a woman.

Get up on that damned horse and head for home. Right now."

She stared at him. The color returned to her face slowly, and her mouth turned firm with determination. Her eyes took on a mocking quality that he'd noticed in them of late. She grinned at him recklessly, and got to her feet, brushing dust from her clothes. She said deliberately, "Make me."

She was a small girl, smaller even than Carrie. She wore a man's wool trousers and a plaid wool shirt. Both were far too big for her. She might have been as skinny as Johnny Sauls for all the clothes revealed. But Clyde knew she wasn't skinny. Not Lacy Quaintance.

He forced a patience he didn't feel into his voice. "Lacy, listen. I haven't got time to wrestle with you." He felt himself coloring, and it angered him. The tiny smile that filled out her lips, and the mocking twinkle in her eyes didn't help either. But behind her amusement and teasing, he sensed a certain dead seriousness. She said firmly, "Then I'm going with you."

"You know what Carrie . . ."

"Damn Carrie! She shouldn't have sent you three off in the first place."

"She didn't send us. Nobody forced us into this."

Lacy laughed without amusement. "No, of course not. Why are men so darn blind?"

He said stubbornly, "You're going back."

Lacy laughed. “Are you going to take me back?” He thought her voice sounded hopeful.

“You know I can’t do that. There isn’t time.”

“Then I’m going. And that’s that.”

She had him, he thought, and she damn well knew it. Two days of travel lay behind—four days if he took her back and returned. The battle north of the White River would be over. The Utes would be streaming back to their camps in the south.

Lacy was watching him. There was something disturbing in the way she looked at him. He turned his glance away uneasily. “All right. You win,” he growled irritably.

He walked over to where her horse stood, cropping grass from the sides of the gully. He hesitated for an instant, about to lead the horse back to her. Then, stubbornness and perversity, along with futile anger, welled up in him.

With a little shrug, he walked back toward camp. He left Lacy to catch her own horse, mount and ride after him.

Stalking furiously along, he was puzzled at himself. A moment ago he’d been thinking of Lacy as a woman, not as Carrie’s younger sister. He suspected that she’d deliberately tried to make him do so too.

And what did she mean by that remark about men being blind? He didn’t know. Scowling, he began to hurry.

CHAPTER 3

LACY QUAINTANCE watched Clyde stride away. She had gained her point, but there was no sense of victory in her. She felt mean, aware that she had added another worry to Clyde's already overburdened mind.

Suddenly tears burned behind her eyes. She didn't want to add to his troubles, or to jeopardize the task he had undertaken. She only wanted to . . . She frowned, trying to understand herself. Exactly what did she want?

She realized that she hoped to change Clyde's mind, to try and turn him back. And if she could not do that, then she wanted to be with him, to share his danger and perhaps even death, if it came. She did not want to exist in a world that did not contain Clyde.

She walked to her horse and mounted lightly. Then she turned the animal in the direction Clyde had gone. Her eyes fixed themselves on his back, and, noting the set of it, she smiled faintly.

He was so stubborn. When he set his mind to something he was as immovable as a rock. And he worshipped Carrie. Damn!

Lacy herself had little memory of the war years. She did remember the great house burning, and afterwards smoldering while they camped around a fire on the lawn. She remembered the hunger and weariness of the long trek west.

But most of her memories were more recent, and concerned with life in the town of Indian Creek. She could not recall a time when she had not loved Clyde; nor could she remember his ever being anything toward her but a kindly, indulgent big brother.

Tears welled into her eyes, brightening them. She brushed them away furiously. She'd not let him see her cry.

When she regained control of herself, she touched her horse's sides with her heels. He broke into a trot.

Catching up with Clyde, she reined the horse deliberately toward him. The horse's shoulder nudged him and made him stagger aside. He looked up, and their eyes met. Suddenly he was grinning at her. "Brat. You did that on purpose." A certain wry maliciousness came into his glance. He said, "If you're going along—and I don't see how I can stop you—you're going to get a haircut."

Dismay touched Lacy's heart. A hand went up automatically to touch her long, shining hair.

Clyde saw the gesture and the expression in her eyes. He said defensively, "We can't take a chance on having the Utes spot a woman among us. You know that as well as I do."

Lacy glared at him. Then abruptly she dug her heels into her horse's sides and pounded on ahead.

She reined her galloping horse to a halt as she reached the camp. She swung down. Johnny Sauls grinned at her cheerfully. "So it was you! I'll bet Clyde's stormin'."

Rufe smiled his slow smile. "Hello, Lacy."

Johnny took her horse and slid the saddle off. Then he led the animal toward where the others were picketed.

Watching Johnny, and then looking at Rufe's almost vacant smile, Lacy suddenly felt a surge of helpless anger. What kind of woman could, for money, send the three men she loved best into danger that might mean death for them all? And why were men so doggone blind?

Lacy did not minimize what Carrie had done for them all. But Lacy, being a woman, understood the motive behind Carrie's actions, something that none of the others did.

Carrie Quaintance lived in the past, and not in the present at all. Carrie lived for a return to the past, to the social whirl and the luxury she had known in Georgia.

Though she had never confronted Carrie with her knowledge, Lacy had, as she grew up, become gradually aware that Clyde and Rufe meant something strange and unnatural to Carrie. They were not so much people to be loved, as they were her ties with the past. They made it possible for Carrie to continue living in the past. And, in a sense, Lacy was in much the same position.

She suspected that was why Carrie had gone to such incredible lengths to keep them all together, beginning the night they had left Georgia and continuing until now. She also suspected it was the reason Carrie had put off accepting Clyde's proposal of marriage. Carrie didn't love him as a man; she loved him only as something which tied her to the past and made bearable the distasteful kind of life she was now forced to live.

But, Lacy thought bitterly, Carrie was willing to sacrifice any or all of them if by so doing she could obtain the actual substance of the past, the security, the luxury, the position. Thirty thousand dollars would give all these to her.

"But what if they fail, Carrie?" asked Lacy aloud under her breath. "What if they fail and are killed?"

It was a terrifying thought.

Clyde came striding up, and Lacy's eyes searched his face. Why couldn't he see? Why wouldn't he?

Discouragement touched her. He would never see. And she couldn't tell him. She couldn't destroy Carrie in his eyes. Loyalty to Carrie prevented it. Her own love for Clyde also made it impossible. She couldn't be the one to hurt him, even if he never saw the truth.

The grays of dusk sifted down across the land. Clyde knelt beside the pile of wood Johnny and Rufe had gathered and began to build a fire. When he had it lighted and crackling, he turned away and got the deer carcass. He unwrapped it and began to slice it.

Lacy rose and found the skillet. She laid rocks around the fire to set it on. Then she began to fry the meat, her eyes downcast and filled with unhappiness . . .

When the deer carcass was completely cut up, Clyde tossed the bones away into the brush. He watched Lacy moodily. Damn it, she certainly had complicated things. It would have been tough enough, trying to do a ten-man job with no more help than Rufe and Johnny. Being saddled with a woman only made it tougher.

He heard a branch crack and glanced up, startled. His hand dropped to touch the grips of his revolver.

A man was riding in, grinning boldly in a brash friendly manner. His eyes were light, almost yellow, and set close to his shapeless nose. His face was covered with a black beard.

He was a broad and powerfully built man, deep chested and massive. He swung heavily from his horse and walked to the fire. His voice was a hoarse rumble, “Well now, this is what I call a welcome. Venison steaks, by God!”

Clyde stared at him in puzzlement for a moment. There was one possible explanation for the man’s presence: he had followed Lacy all the way from Indian Creek. Clyde looked at Rufe. “You ever see him before?”

Before Rufe could answer, the newcomer rumbled, “Sure he has. He’s seen me in Viereck’s saloon. And that’s why I’m here. It was somethin’ he said. It got me wonderin’.”

Clyde asked, “What did Rufe say?”

The stranger grinned. “Somethin’ about bein’ rich.”

Clyde said, “Look at him. You think he knows what he’s talking about?”

The stranger shrugged his massive shoulders. “Maybe. Maybe not. But I was curious. Seemed funny, all of you heading out in the direction of the reservation. So I says to myself, ‘Les, old hoss, there’s somethin’ up. They’s the smell of money in the air.’ ” He grinned at Clyde. “Now me, I got a nose for money. I can smell it out. What is it? Gold?”

Clyde shook his head.

“What, then? You know of some government money that’s buried in the ruins of the Indian Agency?”

Again Clyde shook his head. “You’re wasting your time.”

The stranger glanced at Lacy. His grin barely escaped being a leer. "All the comforts of home, huh, girlie? Looks like old Les Hawken's nose didn't let him down. Money, an' a pretty woman to make the takin' of it pleasurable. Now I call that . . ."

Clyde's voice was like a whip. "Get on your horse and ride!"

Hawken switched his glance to Clyde. His eyes were suddenly as cold and menacing as those of a wolf. "Now I ain't an unreasonable man. But I ain't goin' to leave. You're up to somethin', bucko, an' I aim to find out what it is. Sure, you can run me out of camp. But you can't keep me from followin' along behind. An' if I follow, I'll find out what you're up to, sure as God made little apples."

Clyde's hands were clenched into fists. But he didn't move. Hawken was right; Clyde could drive him out of camp, but he couldn't keep Hawken from following. And once Hawken discovered what they intended to do, there'd be no keeping him out of it.

He felt Lacy's eyes upon him, and Johnny's, and Rufe's too. They were expecting him to do something, and there was nothing he could do. Unless he was prepared to kill Hawken. And he wasn't. Collecting a debt from the Union government was one thing. Murder was quite another.

He scowled blackly into the fire. Johnny said, his voice high and scared, "Clyde, you can't let him tag along. How do we know . . ."

Clyde said, "We'll have to take the chance." He looked at Hawken, standing spread-legged before the fire looking insolently at Lacy. "You've got my tail in a crack and you know it. All right. Come along. You get a one-fifth share, but by God you'll earn every dollar of it."

Hawken grinned. "That's better, bucko. Now. A one-fifth share of what?"

"Of a thousand cattle. The government's got that many down in the White River Valley. They were put there for the benefit of the Utes. We're going in and gather them up and drive them west into Utah. We'll hole up somewhere and re-brand. When the brands have healed, we'll drive them to the railroad and sell them. They ought to bring at least thirty thousand. Your one-fifth share would be around six."

Hawken's grin spread. But Clyde thought there was something sly in his eyes. Hawken said, "Well now, I knew my nose smelled money! Well, by God!"

Clyde cautioned harshly, "I said you'd earn it and I meant it. Most of the braves are up north fighting the troops from Fort Steele, but that don't mean we won't run into Indians. Likely there'll be parties drifting back from the battle. Chances are there'll be reinforcements heading north. They'll all have to pass through the valley. And we may have to fight."

Hawken accepted the condition with a shrug. "Nothin's free," he said.

"And you'll have to work. Gathering a thousand cattle is no cinch."

Hawken shrugged again.

Clyde persisted, his eyes boring coldly into those of Hawken, "One more thing. I'm the boss. Any time you want it otherwise, you got a fight on your hands."

Hawken laughed as though with genuine amusement. "Sure now. Old Les Hawken ain't greedy."

Clyde studied him carefully. He had formed an instant dislike for Hawken. But it would help their chances, he knew, if they had another man along. He got up and walked to the fire. With his knife, he speared a steak and began to eat. Lacy poured a tin cup full of coffee and brought it to him. She whispered, "Clyde, I'm scared. I don't trust him."

"Neither do I. But there's no way to get rid of him without killing him. We'll have to make the best of it."

She returned to the fire. She poured the rest of the cups full, and each of the other three came for their own. Then Lacy returned to Clyde.

Darkness, full and complete, now lay over the land. Stars winked brightly in the cloudless sky. The air had turned chill, and a breeze stirred in the north. Somewhere a pack of coyotes yammered and bickered briefly. The fire winked and flared, and the steaks Lacy was cooking sizzled in the hot tallow.

Clyde finished and set his cup aside. Lacy had finished eating too, so he settled himself on a rock and called, "Come here, Lacy."

She glanced at him, saw the knife he was whetting, and turned a little pale. But she came obediently and sat down between his knees.

With nothing but a knife, the job was difficult. Sometimes it seemed as though he were cutting living flesh, for Lacy winced with each long lock that fell.

A pile of silky, midnight hair began to grow at his side. He worked determinedly and swiftly, cutting it short around her ears like that of Johnny Sauls.

Her body was warm and soft against his knees and he was relieved when the job was done. He said, "There. It's finished."

He stood up and she scrambled to her feet. He turned her around. He was looking critically at her hair, but he couldn't miss the sparkle of tears in her dark eyes. He steeled himself against that and turned away. Damn it, she hadn't had to come.

He went over and squatted beside the fire. He felt ashamed, as though he had done something unnecessarily cruel.

Lacy wandered off outside the circle of firelight and he let her go, knowing she was crying. He turned the steaks absently with his knife. Rufe and Johnny squatted across the fire from him. Hawken stood at the edge of the circle of firelight watching them, an odd expression in his eyes.

Damn a man with a beard, thought Clyde. You could never tell what kind of an expression was on his face. It gave him an advantage in a game like this.

After a while, Lacy returned. There were no tears in her eyes now. She looked at Clyde soberly. "I don't mind, Clyde. Honest I don't. I'm just being silly about it."

Because he felt sorry for what he had had to do, his voice was unnecessarily harsh. "It'll grow back out."

"Of course it will."

He got his blankets and carried them, together with his saddle, out about fifty feet from the fire. He wrapped his blankets around him and lay down, pillowing his head on his saddle. He closed his eyes, but he kept himself facing toward the fire.

Hawken tried to strike up a conversation with Lacy, and Clyde listened to his words, finding nothing in the words themselves to which he could take exception, but finding Hawken's tone suggestive and insulting. He waited, his body strangely tense.

Rufe and Johnny got their blankets and went off a little way from the fire, where they settled themselves to sleep. Lacy finished frying the venison, and put the last of it carefully on a flat rock to cool. Then she too went to get her blankets.

Tension increased in Clyde. Casually, Hawken led his horse toward where the others were picketed, which also happened to be the direction Lacy had gone.

Clyde eased himself out of his blankets. He faded into the shadows beyond the circle of firelight. He headed silently in the direction Lacy had gone.

She could take care of herself, he supposed. She did not need his help. But if he didn't settle this particular point right now it would be cropping up over and over all the way to Utah.

He heard Hawken's low voice, "C'mon now, girlie. Don't be so uppity. All old Les wants is one little kiss. That ain't gonna hurt no one."

He heard the sound of Lacy's palm striking Hawken's face, and afterward Hawken's angry, muffled curse. He heard the brief sounds of a scuffle. . . .

He leaped forward toward the sounds.

CHAPTER 4

BY THE cold light of the stars overhead he saw them.

Hawken's horse had spooked, and now, from a distance, watched the pair with laid-back ears. Hawken had Lacy in his arms. She was struggling, turning her head from side to side, trying to avoid his kiss.

Sudden fury blazed in Clyde. Reaching them, he clubbed Hawken on the ear with his clenched fist. The man's head fell aside with the force of the blow, and he released Lacy instantly. She fell, and rose, and stood watching breathlessly.

Hawken backed away, crouching. His voice rumbled out, "Damn you! You want everything for yourself?"

Clyde lunged. His fist smashed hard against Hawken's mouth. He felt the teeth give beneath it. Hawken stepped back to retain his balance, and shook his ponderous head.

Then he came rushing at Clyde, his head low. Clyde stepped lightly aside, and as Hawken went past, brought his right elbow viciously down against the back of Hawken's neck. Hawken plunged on, off balance, and drove headlong into a thick clump of high sagebrush.

Clyde followed. Hawken came backing out of the brush, but before he could gain his feet, Clyde booted him hard on the rump and drove his head back into the brush.

He backed away warily then, and waited for Hawken to recover. From here on, it was Hawken's choice. He could quit if he wished—or fight it out. Clyde didn't care.

A little core of fury was growing in his brain. Half crouched, he waited.

Hawken came lumbering toward him, ponderous as a bear. His speech was thick. "You hadn't ought to have done that, bucko."

Clyde said, "A warning. Keep away from her."

Hawken laughed. "We'll see. We'll see."

Clyde backed, not to avoid Hawken, but to reach the circle of firelight. And Hawken followed. In the first rays of firelight that struck him, Clyde saw an expression of triumph on his ugly face. Apparently Hawken thought he had Clyde on the run.

Short of the fire by twenty feet, Clyde stopped. And waited, his hands hanging at his sides.

A savage chuckle rumbled from Hawken's throat. His eyes were yellow as brass in the light from the fire—and ugly with promise.

But he came in cautiously, having learned to respect the force behind Clyde's fists. He began to circle, crouching a little, his thick arms held away from his body, his hands widespread.

The stance told Clyde the manner in which Hawken was accustomed to fight. Hawken wanted to fight in close, to break Clyde with his powerful hands and arms.

Clyde leaped in, slashing with right and left at Hawken's face. Blood spurted from a cut his fists opened over Hawken's right eye. He leaped back, and as Hawken lumbered in pursuit, stopped and slashed again.

Rage glittered in Hawken's eyes, and the triumph was gone. He rushed, abandoning caution. With his arms spread to seize Clyde, he presented an open target.

Clyde set himself. As Hawken came in, he swung his right with all the force of his body weight and shoulder muscles behind it. But he swung it low so that it sank into Hawken's bulging midsection.

A burst of air drove out of Hawken's open mouth. His face took on a look of blank surprise. He sat down heavily.

His hand shot to the gun at his thigh, and he yanked it clear.

Clyde stepped toward him and kicked it out of his hand. It discharged from the force of the kick. The bullet flew off harmlessly into the darkness.

A wordless roar of fury burst from Hawken's mouth. He put his hands on the ground and came to his feet in a running lunge. He drove at Clyde, whose back was now to the fire.

Clyde's throat burned from his quickened breathing. He knew he could club Hawken until he broke his hands and never knock the man out. He knew if the fight went on, Hawken would wear him down, and end up breaking his back.

He stood his ground until it seemed certain that Hawken's huge, grasping hands would close on his body. Then he leaped back, and to one side.

Hawken charged past like an enraged bull. Clyde stuck a foot out and tripped him. He whirled, then, to follow, to dive upon the bigger man as soon as he hit the ground—to boot him, knee him, anything that would knock him out.

But there was no need. Hawken fell, sprawling. A wild, savage scream of fear was torn from his lips as he realized that he would plunge face first into the leaping flames and red-hot embers of the fire.

He flung out his hands to break his fall, to save his face. They sank to the wrists in the glowing coals. Sparks flew up in a shower, and a terrible scream burst from the man—a scream of agony that was horrible to hear.

The frantic man rolled from the fire. His shoulder plunged into it as he did, his coat caught fire, and he seemed some kind of fiendish human torch as he continued to roll away from the blaze.

Rufe and Johnny had jumped up from their blankets at the sound of fighting and now stood staring at Hawken, their mouths hanging open. Lacy gasped with horror.

Clyde seized the half-filled coffee pot sitting beside the scattered fire. He dumped it, grounds and all, on Hawken's still burning coat.

There was nothing of the baleful anger in Hawken's face now. Only shock and terror. He held his hands up in the air. They seemed like blackened claws.

Lacy grabbed up the frying pan, in which there was a quarter inch of venison tallow. She scooped out a handful of it and went to Hawken. Trembling and white-faced, he held out his hands to her, struggling up to a sitting position. He winced as she gently spread the grease over them. By the time she had finished, his face was a ghastly gray.

Clyde studied her, marveling. Her face, as she had worked on Hawken's hands, had been as gentle as though she were doctoring a hurt child.

She got up, then, and crossed to where her saddle lay. She took a slicker-wrapped bundle from behind it and unrolled it on the ground. Clyde's eyes widened with surprise. She had a dress and petticoat in the bundle.

She tore some strips from the petticoat, went over and bandaged Hawken's hands. Then she carefully rewrapped the dress and mutilated petticoat, and put them back behind the cantle of her saddle.

Johnny Sauls spoke, his voice breaking on a high note, "Clyde, don't let him come with us! He'll cut our throats first chance he gets!"

Clyde looked across at Johnny. He said gently, "You know a better way, Kid? If we turn him loose, he'll either go back to town and put the law on us, or he'll follow along and make trouble. Best place for him is with us—where we can watch him."

Johnny's voice was shrill. "Then kill him! Kill the . . ."

Clyde shook his head. "You don't mean that."

Johnny was silent. Clyde glanced at Hawken, and saw in the man's eyes a look of hatred so virulent that it seemed to reach out for him. And Clyde realized that in a way Hawken had won, after all. He couldn't kill the man; he couldn't send him back. And he didn't dare drive Hawken out of camp because he knew that Hawken would follow and kill when it pleased him.

He stared at the man on the ground. Hawken outweighed him by nearly forty pounds. He was an animal, a greedy, rapacious animal. He'd never be satisfied with a one-fifth share of the loot, if he thought he could get it all.

Clyde shrugged. Now that the question of Lacy was settled, he doubted if Hawken would present much of a threat—at least until they had the cattle and were safely through the reservation.

But he couldn't keep the contempt out of his eyes as he watched Hawken struggle painfully to his feet. Where Hawken's neck stuck out above his shirt there was a rim of black hair like a fur collar. An animal, a deadly one.

Clyde said, "All right. It's over for tonight. We all need some sleep." He walked off into the darkness and found Hawken's horse. He off-saddled and picketed the horse with the others. He carried Hawken's saddle back to the fire and flung it down.

He untied the blanket roll from behind it and tossed it on the ground at Hawken's feet. Then he stalked away into the darkness. Reaching his blankets, he sat down on the ground and pulled off his boots. Lacy came timidly to lie down near to him. She called softly, "Good night, Clyde."

He growled a good night, and closed his eyes. He thought of what might be ahead with deep foreboding. Even before the arrival of Lacy and Hawken, he'd been beset with doubts. More than ever he wondered if he would not be smart to call the whole thing off.

Then stubbornness took hold of him, as he remembered the way Carrie had looked, so happy and excited. She'd not been like that in all the years they'd been in Indian Creek. It would be cruel to take her dream away and wantonly destroy it.

Besides, he didn't know that Hawken would make trouble. Perhaps, now that he had beaten the man and thus established the fact that he'd take nothing from him, Hawken would go along and do his share without further trouble. It was possible that with Hawken's and Lacy's help, things would go well. Hawken would be invaluable in case of Indian attack. He was tough and fearless.

Clyde could hear Lacy's breathing from where she slept close by. He caught himself thinking of Carrie again.

She had not been happy, he realized now. She had never known real contentment since the war. His face softened. He wanted to do this for Carrie. She deserved it. She'd sacrificed and done without and worked unendingly, with few complaints, for the past fourteen years.

It was surprising that this hard kind of life hadn't changed her more. But to Clyde she seemed no older than she had in Georgia. Her hands were rough, of course. A few tiny lines had begun to appear in her face. A gray hair or two marred the midnight sheen of her hair. But these things only made her more beautiful. Her lips were full and her eyes were bright. And she'd smile more often when Clyde got back with the money the cattle brought.

Perhaps they'd move to Denver. With thirty thousand dollars, or even with that much, less

Hawken's share, Carrie could have almost anything she wanted—a carriage—a big house—clothes like the ones she used to wear back home.

Thinking of her had a way of stirring Clyde's blood, of making it race hotly through his body. Again he let himself imagine what it would be like, married to Carrie.

He'd first asked her to marry him over four years ago, on his twenty-fourth birthday. Remembering it now, his face flushed in the darkness.

He'd come in unexpectedly, returning from a cattle roundup over in the east end of Middle Park. He was excited and breathless. He'd been offered a steady job with the Turkey Track outfit at forty a month. He'd said, "Carrie, I got a steady job, and I'm in love with you. I want you to marry me."

She'd stared at him unbelievingly for a moment. He'd thought she was close to laughter, but she hadn't laughed.

It had been an eternity before she answered. "Clyde, I'm sorry. I love you, but not like that. To me, you're still a boy."

"Hell's bells, I'm twenty-four."

"I know." She looked at him seriously. "But I'm older than you."

"Only four years," he scoffed. He hesitated, not knowing whether to take her in his arms or not. He said tensely, "I've been in love with you ever since I can remember. I used to walk all the way over to your place in Georgia just on the chance I'd see you. I'll wait a while, Carrie. I'll give you time to get used to the idea. But I won't give up. I'll never give up."

She had kissed him then, lightly, and then she had run from the room.

So he went to work for Turkey Track. He worked there for three years, occasionally seeing Carrie, and each time asking her the same question, each time receiving the same evasive answer.

A year ago, walking in the warm twilight with her, Clyde had suddenly seized her in his arms. He'd deliberately stifled her protest with his lips, and had held her hard against him until her arms slipped up around his neck, until her body responded with a need nearly as great as his own.

"Marry me, Carrie. Now. Tomorrow." He'd whispered urgently.

"Yes, Clyde. Yes."

But when he got her home, she hedged. "Wait until Lacy is married, Clyde. Wait until Johnny is out on his own."

"Why? For God's sake, why?"

"I don't know, Clyde. I don't know!" Her words had been anguished. "I guess I'm afraid. I'm afraid to give in to this life we live. If I ever do, it will never change. If I do, we can never go back!"

"Go back? Where?"

"To Georgia. Or at least to the way things were before."

He felt an instant's pity. He said, "That's past, Carrie. Gone. We can never go back to that. But we can have something better, something different."

"I don't want anything different! I want things like they were back home." She began to cry.

He said soothingly, "Carrie, you can't live in the past. Nobody can. It will never come back."

"Maybe it will. Why can't it? Other people strike it rich. Why couldn't we?"

Now this, these cattle, were Carrie's chance to live as she wanted to live, indeed as she had to live. And Clyde would get them for her if it was the last thing he ever did.

CHAPTER 5

FOR a long time, Les Hawken lay still. He knew he wouldn't sleep tonight, so he didn't even try. Instead he lay staring at the stars, thinking.

His hands had a continuous, flaming sensation of pain. It was as though he held his hands in boiling water and could not withdraw them.

Pain came in waves, sometimes so great as to be nearly intolerable. When those times came, he had to hold his trembling body still with a supreme effort of will to keep from springing, screaming, to his feet. Then the pain would ebb. Or maybe it was only that his mind became used to it after so long a time.

He should have let the damned girl alone, he realized now. He should have gone a little slower. But he'd underestimated that damned Clyde. Hell, during the fight, he hadn't even been able to lay a hand on the man.

A wave of pain came on again and he gritted his teeth and rode it out. When it had passed, he was soaked with sweat and trembling violently.

He abandoned himself to hatred of the man

who had done this to him. He promised himself that Clyde would pay for what he'd done before Les Hawken had finished with him.

A one-fifth share! He chuckled softly to himself. Clyde was mushheaded if he thought he was going to be satisfied with that. But let him think it for now. Let him fool himself until after the cattle had been gathered, until after they'd been pushed on through the Indian Reservation. Time enough then for getting even . . .

And the girl . . . If he played it smart, he could take her too. No matter what he had to do to get the cattle, she wouldn't dare open her mouth about it afterward, because if she accused him she would also be accusing the others, and herself as well.

He frowned in the darkness. There seemed to be a closeness between Clyde and the others beyond that of people engaged in a joint effort. And they were an oddly assorted bunch. A kid. A girl. A half-wit. They must be a family, he decided.

He thought about Clyde, about the readiness that had been in Clyde's eyes as they fought. Clyde was a tough one. Probably he'd never killed a man, but that didn't mean he wouldn't. At any time he might kick his scruples aside and decide Hawken was too dangerous to take along. Hawken would be no match for him with his hands in this condition.

The pain returned and he fought it fiercely. Thirty thousand dollars, his for the taking!

A new suspicion entered his mind. Clyde had agreed too readily to giving him a split. Maybe the man was just using him, figuring to let him go along and do a share of the fighting and the work, and then kill him on the other side of the reservation before he could collect his share.

The more he considered it, the more likely it seemed. Clyde wasn't mushheaded. He wasn't fool enough to think Hawken would be satisfied with a small share. But he also realized, in all likelihood, that he needed Hawken.

Hawken's mouth smiled coldly beneath his beard. All right. Two could play this game. A lot of miles lay ahead, dangerous miles that were infested with hostile Indians and all kinds of hazards. Clyde could meet with an accident, a fatal one. Then Hawken could take over leadership of the party and the girl as well. The others would have to accept him—they'd have no choice.

He was smiling faintly as the sky began to gray in the east.

There was a light covering of frost on the ground in the morning, and the air was chill. Clyde was up and had a fire built before dawn was more than a suggestion of grayness in the east.

He squatted before it, staring moodily into it

and shivering in spite of the heat it gave. He was thinking it was probably the last fire they'd have until the job was done, until they had the cattle driven out of the reservation and across the line in the west. Gloomily and with an odd kind of premonition, he wondered if it was the last fire any of them would see before they died.

He glanced sourly over at Hawken's burly shape. He knew Hawken's type, knew the man was a predatory animal, without conscience or scruple. He knew, too, that he was a fool for letting Hawken come along. And yet, he had no stomach for cold-blooded murder, and, he supposed, he never would have. So he'd have to watch Hawken closely all the time. He must never let himself relax.

Lacy came sleepily and knelt on the ground beside him, closer, perhaps, than was necessary. He looked at her face.

Her lips were loose and full with sleep, her eyes wide. She looked very young this morning, almost like a child. He smiled, and she returned his smile gratefully. "Hello, Clyde. Did you sleep well?"

"I slept. Snatches and dozing is all. It's all I'm likely to get until this is over, but it'll have to do."

She nodded soberly, and glanced at Hawken's still form. "His hands must have hurt him terribly last night. He was tossing and groaning all night."

Clyde grunted, “I can’t manage a hell of a lot of sympathy for him.”

“I could have gotten away from him. He wouldn’t have hurt me.”

He glanced at her, and was mildly surprised to see her coloring. He said, “If I hadn’t stopped that last night, he wouldn’t have given you a minute’s peace. Besides, there was more to it than you. Hawken needed to know who was boss. Now he knows.”

“He won’t forget what you did to him.”

“I don’t want him to.” He paused a moment, then added sternly, “You watch yourself, Lacy. Don’t get caught alone with him.”

The coffee was boiling. Lacy set it off the fire onto the ground and added a little water from the canteen to settle the grounds. Johnny and Rufe came stumbling up to the fire, rubbing sleep out of their eyes. Clyde got up and stirred Hawken’s bulky shape with the toe of his boot. “Come on, Hawken. Roll out.”

Hawken rolled onto his back and stared up at Clyde. His eyes apparently had not been shut at all. He was wide awake.

Clyde’s spine was suddenly colder than it had been before. He’d seen that same look once before when he was hunting. He’d shot a badger and broken its spine. Walking toward it to finish it off, he’d caught it staring at him in exactly the way Hawken was staring. The eyes had held no fear at all—only pain and hate and a promise.

Hawken flung back his blankets and sat up. He winced as he put a hand on the ground to help himself to his feet. The blankets fell back on the ground and he started to stoop and pick them up. Clyde said, "Never mind. I'll get them."

Hawken grunted savagely, "Don't do me any favors, bucko." But he let Clyde pick up the blankets, and he moved toward the fire, holding his bandaged hands together against his belly. The bandages were stained with grease and blood.

Clyde shook out Hawken's blankets and rolled them up. He tied them behind Hawken's saddle.

Lacy was gathering up the meat that had been fried last night and laid out to cool. There appeared to be plenty, along with the other provisions Clyde and Rufe carried, to last several days.

Johnny grabbed a couple of steaks and began to gnaw at them. Rufe and Clyde followed suit. Hawken got a cup of coffee and sipped it sourly, scowling.

Clyde watched him. He realized that the man had many days of pain before him, many days of virtual helplessness. Hawken could ride, and help with the cattle, but he'd be useless for camp chores, for anything that required skill with his hands, including shooting. Unless the hands were less severely burned than Clyde thought they were. Unless they healed faster than he expected.

Or unless Hawken's will was such that he could ignore the pain.

He glanced across at Rufe. Rufe was watching Hawken with plain dislike. It was a dumb, almost animal dislike that showed in Rufe's eyes. But in Johnny's eyes, when they touched Hawken, was fear.

Clyde got himself a couple of chunks of meat and began to eat. He sipped scalding coffee between bites. He felt cold, and dirty, and irritable.

Hell, he'd planned all this out in a way that might have worked. Maybe three wasn't enough to go into the reservation and steal the cattle. But he suspected he'd had a better chance before with three than he now had with five. Now he had to wonder what was in Hawken's sly mind. He had to worry, too, about Lacy's safety, both from the standpoint of Hawken, and the possibility of her being captured by Indians.

Maybe Hawken wouldn't bother Lacy again openly—at least while he was around to protect her. But if anything happened to him . . .

When they had finished eating, he detailed Johnny to help Lacy pack the meat, while he went to see the horses. He examined the hoofs of all of them, and examined their backs for sores. All were in good shape.

He saddled, and led the other horses into camp. Johnny and Rufe saddled for themselves. Clyde saddled for Lacy and Hawken. After that, they mounted up and turned westward again, bearing a little north. Clyde figured he'd strike White River sometime in mid-afternoon, and the reservation boundary at nightfall.

They rode through scrub oak, scrub sage, and an occasional quakie pocket. Later, as they drew nearer the high rim of the plateau, they began to encounter spruce and pine timber, lightened occasionally by golden pockets of quakies which gleamed like jewels in their setting of deep green.

Clyde had rearranged their order of traveling, for safety's sake. Hawken now rode in the lead, his reins looped around his wrist. He favored his hands, moving them back and forth to keep them from touching an occasional spruce bough he could not avoid.

Clyde rode second, and watchfully. Behind him came Rufe, his eyes mostly vacant, but occasionally burning with resentful anger as they touched Hawken's burly back. Rufe worshipped Lacy, and would not soon forget that Hawken had roughly tried to make love to her. After that came Lacy Quaintance, and bringing up the rear, Johnny Sauls. Johnny kept glancing behind him nervously.

Lacy seemed somber, almost sad. She watched Hawken's difficulty with something close to compassion. But mostly she kept her eyes on Clyde's broad back. Occasionally they would brighten with tears at her thoughts.

At noon they reached the escarpment of the plateau, and halted to rest the horses. Clyde walked to the rim and looked over, seeking a rail by which they could descend.

Before him stretched miles of untouched wilderness. Far away he could see the twisting ribbon of silver that was White River. Forty or fifty miles to the north, a plume of smoke arose. A forest fire, touched off by the Utes, he supposed.

The rim itself appeared to be forty or fifty feet high, and dropped away from Clyde's feet in a sheer perpendicular cliff. He wandered along it, and after he had gone about a quarter-mile, discovered a game trail leading off.

It followed a natural shelf for the first twenty-five feet of the descent. Then it struck a washout, where water had undoubtedly cut the solid rock in ages past. Brush grew in the washout, making possible the descent, though it was very steep.

He returned to the others. Rufe was glaring at Hawken, and on Hawken's lips was a faint, sardonic smile. Lacy's face was pink.

Clyde didn't need to be told what had been happening. Hawken had been needling Lacy, perhaps subtly enough so that neither Rufe nor Johnny could take open offense, yet needling her just the same in terms all four could understand.

He said harshly, "All right. Mount up and let's go."

He swung to his own saddle and watched the others while they mounted up. He said, "I'll lead. The trail's liable to be tricky for a man without the use of his hands. Hawken, you follow me. Lacy, you bring up in the rear."

He headed out, and a few minutes later reached the head of the game trail leading off the rim.

He edged his reluctant horse forward. The animal danced a few moments at the edge of the brink, but Clyde held him solidly, and at last touched his ribs lightly with the spurs. The horse stepped gingerly onto the shelf.

Clyde swung his head. "Come on, Hawken. Rufe, crowd Hawken's horse a little."

He swung his head back. His leg was scraping the side of the cliff, forcing his horse to the edge of the shelf. The horse began to scramble forward desperately.

Clyde yanked his foot out of the stirrup and raised his leg. The horse edged gingerly in against the cliff, his ears laid back nervously.

Clyde started to swing his head again. He heard a scrambling behind him, and suddenly Hawken's horse rammed hard into his own.

Clyde's mount automatically set his feet as a brake against the unexpected push from behind. Clyde yelled, "Hawken, damn you!"

The head of Hawken's horse slid between the rump of Clyde's and the cliff face. Clyde felt his own horse fighting beneath him, fighting the wedge of horseflesh that was forcing his hindquarters over the edge.

Clyde himself was perched precariously in his saddle, with but one foot hooked in the stirrup. He glanced over the edge at the sheer drop of more than thirty feet to the broken rock below.

With his right foot, which was still in the stirrup, he spurred savagely. His horse seemed to squat under him, then lunged ahead.

But it was too late. The head and neck of Hawken's horse had pushed forward and were between Clyde's horse and the face of the cliff. Both horses were moving forward fast, scrambling like cats along the ledge.

Clyde half swung in the saddle, moving deliberately so as not to upset the precarious balance his horse seemed to be maintaining. He saw Hawken's triumphant expression, and anger soared in his brain. With the ends of his reins he cut Hawken's horse savagely across the nose.

The animal threw up his head, his eyes rolling until Clyde could see their whites. His ears went back and he set his feet blindly.

Clyde's horse lost his footing, thrown off balance by the sudden withdrawal of pressure from behind. His right foot, stepping forward, came down on empty air.

The horse lurched, fighting desperately for balance. And Clyde almost stopped breathing.

The horse's hindquarters went down. He tried

frantically to shift his weight to his left leg, which was still on the ledge.

Looking down, Clyde saw that the washout was now only ten feet below him.

Without hesitation, he jumped, hoping that by leaving the horse he would help the animal to regain his footing on the ledge. He prayed dumbly that the horse's thousand pounds of kicking, fighting weight would not come plummeting down on top of him before he could scramble out of the way.

In his ears was the long, lost sound of Lacy's scream, and then he hit. His left leg struck first, going out from under him with a binding flash of pain. He was rolling, and being clawed by brush as he tumbled end over end down the steep grade toward the bottom of the washout.

The noise of his descent was a continuous roaring in his ears. But he was listening, almost breathlessly, for the crash above that would tell him his horse had fallen too and was now rolling down on top of him.

He came to rest against a thick clump of brush, and for a moment lay there, too stunned to move. Then he got to his feet, favoring the left leg, which was burning fiercely with pain. He looked up.

His horse had recovered, and now was nervously picking his way from the ledge to the washout. Hawken came along behind.

In back of Hawken, the faces of Johnny and

Rufe were bloodless. But it was Lacy's expression that caught and held Clyde's eyes. Her lips were moving soundlessly, and her eyes were wide and filled with an awful kind of fear. Clyde grinned shakily at her. "It's all right, Lacy," he called. "Come on down. But be careful."

He stepped aside as his horse reached him, and took the reins. Gritting his teeth against the pain, he jammed his left foot into the stirrup and swung astride. When he hit the saddle, his face broke out into a cold, clammy sweat.

He looked down at his leg, and automatically ran his hand along his thigh. Badly wrenched, but not broken, he guessed. Damn Hawken!

Clyde swung his head. Hawken's reins were still hooked around his wrist. His eyes were without expression.

Clyde turned away. It *could* have been an accident. Hawken had very little control over his horse without the use of his hands. But instinct told Clyde it had been no accident; it warned him that he had better be wary of Hawken in the days to come.

It also reassured him in one respect—Hawken would not try to kill him openly. It would look like an accident when it happened. For only by making it appear so would Hawken be able to assume leadership of the party. The others would never accept him.

CHAPTER 6

THEY HALTED soon afterward. Clyde's leg was a steady, throbbing ache.

He dismounted stiffly, hobbled over to a rock and sat down. Lacy brought him some cold meat. She said, "Are you sure it isn't broken, Clyde?"

He nodded. "Wrenched, is all."

Johnny went around collecting canteens. When he had them all, he refilled them from a narrow, tumbling stream nearby. He brought Clyde's to him and Clyde took a long drink. Then he studied the little group carefully.

Lacy sat on a rock, staring at nothing. Hawken watched her covertly, his eyes alive. Rufe Thebus stared at Hawken with a deep continuing hatred unusual in this slow-witted man. Johnny Sauls kept trembling, as if he were cold. He stared at the ground between his feet, apparently immersed in his own thoughts and fears.

Clyde felt like a commander entering enemy territory with untrained, untried troops. He knew he couldn't count on them. He could only hope that from somewhere in the depths of each would come the strength that was needed when the time came.

Rufe would probably be all right as long as he didn't have to think for himself, as long as Clyde was near to give him orders and instructions. Johnny was an unknown quantity; he might break completely when stress came, or he might come through. Lacy might be of help in handling the cattle, but she must be protected in any fighting that might develop. And Hawken . . . Clyde frowned. Hawken must be watched constantly. Clyde was convinced that the incident on the shelf trail had been no accident, even though it might have looked like one.

Apparently Hawken felt Clyde's steady regard, for he switched his own glance from Lacy to Clyde. There was an unfathomable, mocking humor in his eyes. His expression dared Clyde to prove that his fall had been anything but an accident.

Clyde said, "Rufe, you were right behind Hawken up there on the rim. What happened?"

Rufe pulled his eyes away from Hawken with an effort. He cleared his throat. "You told me to crowd his horse into the trail, so I did. But I didn't crowd him into you, Clyde. Honest I didn't."

"Nobody said you did, Rufe. I know better than to think that."

"He did it, Clyde. Hawken did it."

"How do you know that?"

"He was usin' his spurs."

Hawken broke in angrily. "Sure I was. I was tryin' to get the damn bronc to take that trail." He got up and walked toward Rufe. He looked down threateningly. "What're you tryin' to say, stupid? That I tried to push Valle's horse off the trail? That I did it on purpose?"

Rufe lifted his head. There was an expression of dumb fright on his face. Clyde had the odd impression that it wasn't exactly physical fright, either. It was confusion, and troubled uneasiness because his own mind wouldn't keep up with Hawken's. Rufe muttered, defiantly, "You was usin' your spurs. I saw you."

Clyde broke in, "Never mind. Never mind. It's over, and nobody's killed. Let's get goin'."

Rufe and Johnny got up and started for their horses. Suddenly Rufe stumbled and fell headlong. The slope was steep and he rolled for several feet before he came to rest in a patch of prickly pear. He howled, and rolled clear. Hawken, above him, began to laugh. He asked, "Trip over your own big feet stupid?"

Anger soared in Clyde. He understood Hawken's motive for this. Hawken was trying to intimidate Rufe. Hawken's crowding of Clyde's horse back on the rim had been a deliberate attempt to kill Clyde, and Rufe knew it. Hawken probably realized that if he did not thoroughly frighten Rufe now, the man would refuse to accept him later as the party's leader.

Rufe's eyes were tormented. He launched himself up the steep slope at Hawken, scrambling on hands and knees. Clyde could see spines of prickly pear on the left side of his face and on his hands.

Hawken put his weight on his left leg, readying the right one to kick. Clyde drew his gun and put a bullet into the ground at Hawken's feet. He said, "You kick Rufe, and I'll put the next one in your head."

Hawken settled back solidly on both feet. Rufe had stopped, and now struggled to a standing position. Clyde said, "Help him pull out those damn cactus spines, Lacy."

Lacy went over and gently began to pull the spines. Rufe's eyes watched her with an expression that stirred pity in Clyde's heart. He walked over to Hawken. "Keep pushing, you bastard. Keep it up and you'll get a slug in your brisket."

Hawken turned sullenly and got his horse. He mounted and sat waiting impatiently. He didn't look at Clyde again.

Clyde went to his own horse and tightened the cinch. He mounted. Lacy had finished with Rufe. Now she caught her horse and mounted, watching Clyde. Her eyes seemed to be probing, weighing the things she saw in his face.

Her expression disturbed him. It was as if

she was searching him for change, as if she was trying to decide how far he would go with Hawken.

The trouble was he didn't know himself. But he recognized the pressures that were on him. He was worried about the safety of Lacy and Johnny and Rufe. He realized that Hawken was a threat to them all.

So far, he hadn't reached the point where he was willing to kill. But Lacy was wondering if he had.

When everyone was mounted, Clyde spoke to Hawken. "Lead out."

Hawken scowled, but he complied without protest. This afternoon, he held the reins in his bandaged left hand. He held them gingerly, and occasionally winced with pain. Clyde debated taking his gun away from him, and then post-poned deciding the question.

They wound steadily downward, following first one drainage and then another. They saw game often, but neither tracks nor signs of other human beings. In mid-afternoon, they came over a long ridge and dropped at last into the White River Valley.

Clyde's tension increased at once, and he halted the column while he studied the yonder slope and the reaches of the river, both upstream and down. He froze when he saw two horsemen picking their way along at the foot of the ridge.

He watched them intently. When they turned right and disappeared into the timber, heading directly toward him, he eased his gun out of its holster and thumbed back the hammer. He said softly, "Hawken, I've got a gun on you. Ease your rifle out of the boot and let it slide to the ground."

Hawken's back stiffened. For a long moment he sat utterly still. Then, slowly, he slipped his rifle from under his left leg and let it drop.

Clyde said softly, "Now your six-shooter."

Hawken hesitated.

Clyde said warningly, "Don't try it, Hawken. Just let it slide to the ground."

Hawken complied. Then he swung his head and looked at Clyde. "You son of a bitch!"

Clyde smiled grimly. "Now move on—about ten feet."

Hawken obeyed. Clyde returned his own gun to its holster as he said, "Johnny, get his guns and hand them up to me."

Johnny rode past him, dismounted and picked up the guns. Clyde shoved the revolver into his belt and held the rifle in his hands, resting it across his saddle.

Johnny looked up. "What're we goin' to do, Clyde, who are they?"

"I don't know. We'll wait and see."

He waited, watching Hawken. After what seemed an interminable time, the two strangers emerged from the timber and climbed the ridge toward them.

They were white men, and both rode what appeared to be extremely fine mounts. One of the riders was light-haired, with a beard that was clipped and neat. The other was thin-faced, with a stubble of reddish whiskers on his face.

They eyed the little group with amazement. The bearded one exclaimed, "I'll be damned! Where do you think you're goin'?"

Clyde didn't answer.

The man said, "You know you're headin' into the reservation, don't you?"

Clyde nodded. "We're headed for Utah."

"You'll never make it. Not unless you swing north and go around."

Clyde said, "Maybe that's what we'll do."

"Haven't you heard the news?"

"You mean about the Ute uprising?"

"Uh-huh. There's three thousand of 'em up north of here. They've got Major Thornburg and his men pinned down—killed all their horses. Somebody got out and fetched some colored troops from Middle Park, but they're no better off. While they were ridin' in, the Utes picked off every damned one of their horses too."

Clyde shrugged. He asked, "Were you with Thornburg?"

"Not likely." The man rode close to Clyde and stuck out his hand. "Whitey Blake. This here's

Hal Arnold." He grinned. "Hal and me make a livin' out of horseracin' with the Utes."

"Horse racing?"

"Yeah." He patted his horse's neck. "A Ute brave will bet anything—even his squaw—on a horse race. Hal and me just cash in on it."

Clyde said, "Where is this fight you mentioned?"

Whitey said, "Milk River. You keep straight north and you'll miss it; but don't swing west. You're dead if you do."

Clyde said, "Move out, Hawken." He spoke to Blake. "Thanks for the warning."

The man shrugged. "It's all right. Good luck."

Clyde followed Hawken down the slope. He had gone about twenty yards before he swung his head. Both Blake and Arnold were looking at Lacy. Clyde shouted irritably, "Come on, kid. Move."

But somehow, as he moved away, he did not think he had fooled them. They knew Lacy was a girl. It was in their eyes as they watched her ride down the slope.

When they were out of earshot, Johnny asked breathlessly, "You reckon they'll follow us, Clyde?"

"I don't know."

"What'll we do if they follow us?"

Clyde glanced back at him impatiently. "How do I know what we'll do? It depends on what they do."

"I was just wonderin'." Johnny lapsed into silence.

Clyde urged his mount on and moved ahead of Hawken. With the man disarmed, he need no longer fear Hawken's treachery. At least not here. Hawken fell in behind him and Johnny Sauls followed. Behind Johnny rode Lacy, and Rufe brought up the rear.

It was a beautiful valley that lay before Clyde's eyes. In some places it pinched down, until the sparkling, tumbling river ran between narrow canyon walls, but in others it widened to almost half a mile. Where it did, there were meadows, lush with native grass that was belly deep on a horse. Some day these would be hay meadows, thought Clyde, dotted with cabins and with brown stacks of hay and cattle grazing around them.

There would be trout in that stream, an abundance of them, for Indians seldom fished. There would be game on the hillsides for a man's taking.

Clyde felt a sudden surge of emotion that was almost like homesickness. A man who lived here would have everything that a man would want. He could raise his children strong and healthy and glad to be alive. He could lie in the scented darkness of night with his woman, and listen to the pleasant roar of the river. . . .

Clyde drove his thoughts away angrily. Such

hopes had no place in his mind. Carrie would want nothing to do with as primitive a place as this. Carrie wanted to be where people were; she wanted a life similar to the one she had known back home.

He put his mind on the task ahead. So far, they had encountered no sign of Indians. But they would soon. It was inevitable. And there were the two horseracers, Blake and Arnold. Clyde turned and scanned his back trail anxiously. He saw nothing.

Hawken was grinning at him maliciously. He said hoarsely, "They were some puzzled by you, Clyde. Wouldn't surprise me if they followed along to see what you was up to."

Clyde scowled, but he didn't answer.

He had no way of knowing where the reservation boundary was. He guessed it didn't matter. What did matter was that from here on they had to be on guard constantly.

He halted for the night at sundown, eyeing a small gulch off to his right. It was a perfect spot to camp. It overlooked a narrow spot in the valley, and was amply screened by trees. A tiny stream tumbled from it, and Clyde knew there would be plenty of feed among the trees for the picketed horses.

He swung in his saddle and gestured toward the gulch.

He thought Lacy looked wan and tired tonight.

Hawken was scowling. Johnny's face was expressionless, and Rufe seemed befuddled.

They all turned their horses and rode obediently into the gulch. Clyde followed.

They had a campsite picked out about a hundred yards up the gulch when he arrived. Each was unsaddling. When they had finished, Johnny took their horses and led them up the gulch to picket them out for the night.

Clyde made no move to dismount. He looked at Lacy, aware suddenly how often his thoughts turned to her, depended on her. He said, "I'm going to scout around down-river until dark. I'd like to know what we're getting into."

Sudden concern leaped into her eyes. Her face was grimy and there was a smudge on her cheek. She combed her fingers through her short hair in an automatic gesture. "Be careful."

He nodded and rode away, and a moment later disappeared into the trees.

Rufe immediately went off to gather sticks for a fire, but Lacy called him back. "Clyde said no fire, Rufe."

"Oh, I forget." Rufe came back and sat down on a rock. His eyes were blank tonight, almost empty. Lacy shook her head slightly as she went to the stream where she washed her face and hands. She got a brush out of her saddlebags and began to brush her short-cropped hair. She wouldn't look at Hawken, but she knew he was looking at her. An odd uneasiness possessed her, and afterwards she stayed near her saddle, where her rifle was.

Johnny returned after a few moments. He dipped his hands into the stream, passed them over his face, then came and sat down near to Lacy. She could sense his nervousness even before he spoke. "You think we'll see Injuns tomorrow, Lacy?"

"Maybe. I don't know, Johnny. Stop worrying about it."

"Yeah."

Silence ran on, silence that Hawken finally broke. "You sure as hell better hope we don't see no Injuns, kid. They've all gone wild, like they did out on the plains durin' the war. I seen a ranch they raided once, on my way out here. The buildings were all burned. There was some stock in the barn when they set it afire, an' the air was thick with the smell of scorched meat and burnt hair."

Lacy said tightly, "Be quiet. We don't want to hear about it."

He looked at her with exaggerated innocence. "Just talkin' to pass the time. What's the harm of that?" He glanced at Johnny. "Besides, you ought to know what's comin', because Clyde won't tell you. He's afraid you'll quit." After a moment he went on. "Out in the yard, we found the people. The woman and two gals was stark naked, an' their hair was gone. Man was sittin' on the ground like he'd been buried alive . . ."

Lacy suddenly felt ill. The color had drained from her face, leaving it ghastly gray. Johnny jumped to his feet. His voice was high and unstable. "God damn it, shut up! What you tryin' to do?" His voice broke. "Shut up, you hear?"

Hawken looked at him aggrievedly. "Why sure, Johnny. No call to get riled. I just thought you folks ought to know what's comin'. I figured you ought to know what goddam animals them Injuns are, so's you won't be tempted to treat 'em like humans."

"What do you mean by that?" Lacy asked.

Hawken shrugged elaborately. He said with seeming reluctance, "I was thinkin' about Clyde. There ain't enough sand in him to pull this off. If there had been, he'd have killed me, or tried, the night I walked into camp."

"You ought to be glad he didn't, instead of criticizing him for it."

"Oh, I'm grateful; it's just . . ."

Johnny yelled, "You shut up. You shut up, or . . ."

"Or what?"

Johnny yanked his rifle from the saddle scabbard beside him. He levered a shell into the chamber and swung the rifle around. He whispered breathlessly, "Or I'll do what Clyde didn't!"

Hawken chuckled contemptuously. Lacy looked at him and shuddered. She knew without doubt that he had deliberately thrown out that Indian story to unnerve Johnny and undermine Clyde.

She said, "Put that gun down, Johnny."

Johnny put it down sullenly. He growled, "Why doesn't Clyde get back? What the hell's he doin', anyway?"

Hawken said smoothly, "He's scouting for Indians. Could be they got him already. Could be they got him staked out on the ground or tied to a tree, an' are stickin' flamin' sticks into his belly. Or they might've left that till later, an' right now be followin' his tracks right back to us."

Johnny glanced at him angrily, but Lacy could see the way his eyes pinched down with fear. He ran up the slope of the gulch and peered out into the valley and down-river. In a moment he returned.

Lacy said steadily, "Johnny, you're doing exactly what he wants you to do. You're letting him panic you."

He scowled fiercely, but his lower lip was trembling. "Well, hell! What am I supposed to do?"

Lacy said, "Don't listen to Hawken. He's just trying to scare you." She started to tell Johnny why, then stopped herself. Telling him would only scare him worse.

But she knew. Hawken intended to get rid of

Clyde. He'd tried it once already. And if he did, he wanted every member of the party so terrified that they'd accept his leadership out of desperation.

He'd use them, then, until the cattle had been driven out of the reservation; then he'd take the cattle for himself. She felt a touch of terror. If he succeeded in killing Clyde, there was nothing on earth any of them could do to stop him, short of . . .

Lacy realized she was trembling. She had never contemplated killing a man, but she was contemplating it now. And she knew she'd do it if she had to—without any hesitation at all.

CHAPTER 7

THE LITTLE STREAM made a pleasant, rushing sound as it tumbled down the gulch. The sun was down now, but its afterglow remained on a few high and scattered clouds. A magpie flew overhead and started to light in one of the trees nearby, but the bird saw the men beneath it and veered away. Hawken cursed softly under his breath. These were the signs the Indians watched, and if an Indian had been watching that magpie, he'd know for sure that something or someone was hidden in these trees.

He watched Lacy and Johnny covertly as they talked quietly together. He couldn't hear what they said, but he knew he had frightened them both with his talk of Indian atrocities.

Knowing there would be no light when the day was gone, Hawken began awkwardly to peel the bandages off his hands. He untied the knot on the right-hand bandage with his teeth, and then unwound it carefully. When the bandage was off, he looked at the hand critically. He couldn't afford to be without the use of his hands during the next few days. This was the biggest opportunity that had ever come his way, and he intended to take full advantage of it.

The hand was not as badly burned as he had feared it was. The back of it wasn't burned at all. Just singed. He turned it over and looked at the palm.

The grease had loosened the black soot from the palm, and had helped it be absorbed by the bandage. The hand, fairly clean now, was a mass of blisters, some of which had broken. That accounted for the blood on the bandage. It would hurt like hell to hold a gun, but it wasn't impossible, Hawken decided.

He unwound the bandage on his left hand and looked at it. There wasn't much difference between the two hands so far as the severity of the burns was concerned. One was about as bad as the other. The blisters would give trouble, but if he handled things carefully, he'd get along.

He rewound the bandages meticulously, leaving his fingers free. The sun glow had faded from the clouds and now, at twilight, the land lay silent around him, somehow menacing in its very silence.

He glanced at Lacy and Johnny and Rufe in turn, thinking that this was going to be a hard combination to overcome. Not physically, of course. He could do that any time, easily. The trouble was, he needed these others, needed them to help get the cattle gathered and through the valley. If they only didn't have this family loyalty among them.

Well, he'd have to make the best of it. Johnny's weak point was fear of Indians and youthful uncertainty. Rufe's was his confused, befuddled mind. And Lacy's . . . He frowned. Lacy had no weakness unless it was her love for Clyde. And with Clyde gone . . .

Right, now, Hawken needed a gun. If he had one, he could make the excuse that he was worried about Clyde, go searching for him. He could cut Clyde down out there in the darkness, fire a couple or three more shots to make it sound good, then bring Clyde's body in. They'd believe that Indians had done it—or a lone Indian. Even if they didn't believe it, they wouldn't be able to prove otherwise. And with Clyde gone, they'd be alone here in the reservation, dependent entirely on Hawken's resourcefulness to get them safely out.

Right now if he could get them fighting him and fighting among themselves, perhaps he could get his hands on one of their guns.

He looked across at Johnny. "They tell me there was five or six women down there at the Indian Agency. Likely just enough to whet the appetites of the damned savages." He looked pointedly at Lacy. "Funny the taste Indians get for white women. You'd think they'd prefer their own, wouldn't you? But they don't. Most Indian bucks would pass over the ten prettiest women in the tribe just to get at a white one." He hesitated a moment. "Lacy hadn't ought to be here at all. If the Indians find out she's a woman, there's nothin' in the world can save us."

Lacy and Johnny were trying hard to ignore him, but neither was succeeding. Johnny looked at Lacy. The light was poor, but Hawken thought Johnny's expression was resentful.

His grin spread. "Know what they do when they catch a white woman? They stake her out on the ground. Then they all take turns. If she's strong, and survives, she belongs to the buck that first captured her as soon as they get back to the village. Most likely he'll take her on as another of his wives, but it ain't a very nice life, believe me. The other wives don't like her, and they abuse her every chance they get. First thing you know, that Indian buck's got so damned much wife trouble on account of this one white wench that he's about to go crazy. So he says to hell with it and trades her to someone for a horse."

Hawken could feel Rufe's eyes on him. He turned to stare at the man. Rufe tried angrily to stare him down, but he couldn't do it. He looked away.

Hawken sobered and said persuasively, "It's a damn good thing for all of you that I came along, even if you don't believe it now. I know Indians.

I know how they think. I can get you out of this mess with whole skins if anybody can."

Nobody answered him. He said, in the same persuasive tone, "You all got to look at this the way it is. You need me worse than you've ever needed anything in your lives before. An' I'm willin' to help."

Lacy said contemptuously, "Help!"

"Yes, help. And you sure need it. Look at the three of you. A kid so damn scared he's ready to jump out of his pants. A girl in man's clothes. And a stupid, addle-brained half-wit."

He heard Rufe make a sound like a choked growl. Glancing at him, he saw he had touched Rufe's sore spot with his remark about addled brains.

Lacy said evenly, "You're forgetting Clyde."

"No, I'm not. Clyde's a good man, but not good enough. He ain't hard enough. And he don't know a damn thing about Indians."

He had them listening now, however unwillingly. Their minds were not thinking about Hawken; they were thinking about Indians, and themselves, and Clyde.

He got up and stretched ostentatiously. "Wish we had a fire. It's gettin' cold."

He glanced at Lacy. Her rifle was in the saddle boot on her saddle, which lay at her side. It would be hard to get it out quickly, he realized.

Beyond her, Johnny was sitting on a log.

Johnny's rifle lay beside him, leaned against a log. Across from them sat Rufe on the ground, his rifle under his legs.

Johnny's gun was the only chance. But if he could get it, he knew he could keep it.

He looked up at the sky. It was gray now, and soon it would be dark. Clyde would no doubt return at dark, or soon after. So if Hawken wanted to get him as he came toward camp, he'd better have a try for Johnny's gun—now.

Ignoring the others, he sauntered across the little clearing toward the place where Johnny sat. He had to force himself to keep his eyes off Johnny's rifle and to look at the boy instead.

He made his voice sympathetic. "How old are you, Johnny?"

Johnny looked up. "Fifteen. Why?"

"Nothin'. I was just thinkin' how much of your life's in front of you. All the good part. It ain't right for you to get knocked off now."

"Who said I was goin' to get knocked off?" Johnny's voice was defiant.

"Nobody." Hawken sat down on the log, not close enough to Johnny to frighten him, but close enough so that he could reach the gun by diving for it.

Hawken said, "Guess you think I was tryin' to be ornery, talkin' so much about Indians, don't you?"

Johnny didn't answer, so Hawken went on

persuasively, “You folks got me all wrong. Like that business with Lacy the first night. Like that accident up on the rim. Oh hell, I’ll admit I want a cut of what them cattle bring. But that’s all. Just a fair cut.” Hawken edged just a little closer. “An’ I could help, if you folks would trust me.”

Out of the corner of his eye, he saw Lacy watching him. She said, rising, “Johnny, what’s he whispering about?”

Hawken knew he had to move. In an instant more it would be too late.

He snatched at the rifle. He felt his hand close on its barrel, and he yanked it toward him.

Johnny grabbed for it and got it by the stock. Hawken lunged to his feet and twisted savagely, driven wild by the pain in his hands. The gun came loose from Johnny’s hands and Hawken backed away. He said angrily, “Easy, now! Easy. If Clyde thinks I’m ridin’ through the reservation without a gun, he’s crazy. You can’t blame me for that.”

He saw Johnny dive toward him, reaching for the gun. He brought the muzzle around and cracked Johnny on the side of the head. It was not a knockout blow but it stunned Johnny and knocked him off his feet. Lacy cried, “Johnny, let it go! Let it go! He’ll kill you!”

On his hands and knees, Johnny froze.

Hawken said, “That’s it, kid. Take it easy. I don’t want to hurt anybody. I just want a gun.”

The light was almost gone now from the little clearing. Far off down-river, a pack of wolves howled in chorus and nearer, some coyotes, excited by the sound, began to yap and quarrel among themselves.

Excitement began to rise in Hawken. The first step of his plan had been successfully completed. Now for Clyde.

Johnny was still motionless on the ground. Lacy stood a dozen feet away. Rufe hadn't moved from the place he'd been sitting. But he was moving now, moving and yanking the gun from under him.

Angered, Hawken swung the rifle to cover him. He said sharply, "Rufe, don't do it! I'll shoot!"

Almost any other man but Rufe would have heeded his words, he realized with helpless anger. That was the trouble with someone whose wits were addled. They couldn't add things up. They got their thoughts lined out in a single direction and nothing could alter them.

Rufe had the rifle in his hands now, swinging it around. Hawken, remembering that Johnny had earlier jacked a shell into the chamber, now thumbed back the hammer to full cock. He tried once more, "Rufe! Hold it!" And then he fired.

Powdersmoke billowed from the muzzle, momentarily obscuring his target. He stepped to one side anxiously, and levered another cartridge into the chamber.

But it wasn't necessary. Rufe was on the ground.

Lacy ran toward him. Hawken's voice was like a whip. "Stay where you are!"

Lacy paid no attention. Hawken leaped toward her, and cuffed her roughly aside. Then went over and looked at Rufe.

The man was apparently unconscious. He was not dead. Hawken picked up his rifle and flung it away into the brush. He turned. "All right," he said to Lacy. "Take a look at him."

He felt balked, defeated. He couldn't go after Clyde now. Clyde would have heard the shot. He'd be on guard.

Hawken stared at the dim shapes of Lacy and Johnny, kneeling on the ground beside Rufe. He cursed savagely under his breath. Then he stepped back out of the clearing to wait. Indians might have heard the shot. Clyde certainly had. And Hawken didn't intend to be caught off guard.

Kneeling beside Rufe, Lacy felt a surge of helpless panic. It was almost dark now. Shot or no shot, Indians or no Indians, they had to have a fire or some kind of light. She swung her head toward the shadows. Though she couldn't see Hawken, she knew he was there. She said angrily, "Don't just stand there. Build a fire. I've got to have some light."

She got no reply. Nor could she see him move.

She sprang to her feet. She ran and got Rufe's rifle from where Hawken had flung it at the edge of a clump of brush. She turned. "I'm not fooling. If you don't, either I'm going to shoot you or you're going to have to shoot me. So make up your mind and make it up fast."

Lacy knew she meant what she said, and she hoped he knew it too.

Apparently he did. He came out of the shadows.

"What the hell's the matter with that kid? Let him do it," he growled.

Lacy said, "You do it. I need Johnny."

Johnny got up. "I'll help him. Not much either of us can do till you get some light." He went out into the darkness, which was now nearly complete. Hawken helped him, gathering a few small sticks with his free hand, but not letting go of the rifle. Johnny returned and dumped an arm load of wood beside Rufe. He said breathlessly, "Lacy, you reckon he's hit bad?"

"I don't know. How could I? Hurry up and light that fire." She realized her voice had been sharp, and knew that fear had made it so.

As Johnny piled up a little pyramid of twigs, she glanced into the wall of darkness around her. Had something happened to Clyde? Was that the reason he had not returned? She calmed herself with the thought that if Clyde had run into trouble she'd have heard gunshots. And she'd heard nothing.

Johnny touched a match to his tiny pile of twigs, and as the flames caught, carefully added more wood. Hawken said. “That’s enough! What do you want, a bonfire?”

Lacy knelt beside Rufe. His eyes were open and staring at her, numb with shock and pain. She unbuttoned his jacket and shirt and gently folded them back. Blood, shiny and thick, oozed from a small, ragged hole in the muscles of his shoulder.

She turned her head and spoke to Johnny. “Get a saddle. Then help me lift him.”

Johnny brought a saddle, and between them they eased Rufe back against it until his wounded shoulder was clear of the ground. Lacy was tempted to cut his jacket and shirt away from it, but she didn’t. She knew they had no extra clothes along, and Rufe would need his.

With Johnny’s help, she lifted Rufe to a sitting position. He groaned, and his face twisted with pain. Beads of sweat sprang out on his forehead.

Lacy gritted her teeth. “This is going to hurt, Rufe.”

He tried to smile. “All right, Lacy. Go to it.”

As gently as she could, she took off his jacket and shirt, Johnny holding him upright as she did. Rufe cried out once, sharply, and then fainted. Lacy and Johnny eased him back down on the saddle.

And now, in the flickering fire light, Lacy looked at the wound.

The bullet had gone clear through, making a small hole in front going in, and a ragged, larger one in the back coming out. Apparently it had missed the arteries, because the flow of blood was steady and oozing, rather than spurting.

Lucy ran and got the bundle containing her dress and petticoat from behind her saddle. She unwrapped it and tore some strips from the petticoat. With a small pad made from the petticoat, she dabbed at the back of Rufe's shoulder, looking for bone splinters. Rufe had been lucky. The bullet had also missed the bone.

She put a thick compress in front and back, and bound them on with strips wound around Rufe's shoulder and secured by winding more back and forth to his neck. Then she got to her feet, trembling with exhaustion.

"Get his blankets and one of mine," she told Johnny. "There's nothing more I can do for him right now. He needs rest and sleep."

Johnny got the blankets and Lacy arranged them over Rufe so that he would be comfortable and warm. The fire had died down, and now Hawken came over and began to stamp it out. Lacy said bitterly, "Maybe you'd better keep watch for Indians. Somebody's got to. If any of them heard that shot, they'll surely be here soon."

He walked away without speaking. Lacy sat down, and suddenly she found herself crying—silently and terribly. Back in town Rufe's wound would have not been too serious. A week in bed and a doctor's care would do wonders for him. But he wasn't back in town and there were no doctors. Rufe could rest tonight, but he'd have to be up and in his saddle tomorrow. He'd have to ride all day, and the next day, and the next, until they were safely out of the reservation.

This was turning into a nightmare, Lacy thought frantically.

She calmed herself with a determined effort of will. She picked up Rufe's rifle from the place she'd laid it. With it in her hands, she sat down in the darkness.

At each small noise she heard, she started violently. She began to think that Clyde would never come, and that the night would never end. A premonition of disaster began to grow in her mind.

Hawken, she knew, would try to kill Clyde again—if not tonight, then tomorrow, or the day after that. And what if he succeeded?

She shivered, cold with fear. She remembered Hawken's burly strength, the ugly cruelty of his yellowish eyes, the sly deviousness of the man. She knew she was no match for him. But she could prevent him from killing Clyde tonight. She could listen for Clyde as well as he. And when Clyde came in, she could scream a warning to him. She would do that even if Hawken killed her for it.

CHAPTER 8

UPON LEAVING the others, Clyde Valle had ridden down river slowly and cautiously, staying near the creek and hidden by the willows that grew along its bank. All the while, his eyes roved the slopes to north and south, looking for hostiles, seeking telltale signs that would betray their presence.

He saw nothing, so he continued westward for about five miles. He found several places along the way where he judged Indians had been camped no more than a week before. But he found neither fresh campsites nor fresh tracks, though he saw a number of cattle.

Satisfied, he turned back. So far, things were going well. He and Carrie had guessed right when they'd reached the conclusion that the Indians would evacuate the White River Valley. In anticipation of conflict with the Longknives, they'd moved their villages south, some of them probably as far as Grand River. Their warriors had ridden north to fight the troops.

But Clyde was not deceived by the apparent emptiness of the valley. He knew, as Hawken had known, that wounded would be trickling south in parties of three to a dozen, heading for the safety of the villages. Reinforcements would be traveling north to join the battle. It was said that the Uncompaghre Utes might join their northern brothers in a last-ditch attempt to defeat the whites. Clyde hoped desperately that this would not happen. If it did, he and the others would be overwhelmed and butchered without mercy.

Dusk came down, and light gradually faded from the sky. Clyde, feeling relatively safe now, rode out of the cover of the stream bed and into the open valley, where traveling would be easier and faster. In the soft light of dusk, the valley was even lovelier than it had been before, in sunlight. Several times Clyde paused to stare out across it.

He was still a couple of miles from camp when he heard the shot, loud and sharply clear in the still, cool air.

He halted instantly, and held his breath as he listened. Beneath him, his horse fidgeted nervously.

The silence was not broken again.

Clyde scowled. Had Indians attacked the little group in the gulch? It wasn't likely. If they had, there would have been a number of shots by now, unless those in camp had been taken by surprise. But even if it were not an attack, the sound of that shot might carry for miles. And if any hostiles happened to be within hearing distance they were sure to investigate.

Clyde felt irritation mounting in him. It could have been a careless, accidental shot, but it could have been something else. Hawken was vicious and dangerous. Perhaps he had managed to get his hands on one of the guns. He might have shot either Johnny or Rufe. He might even have hurt Lacy.

At the thought of that, Clyde sank his spurs suddenly and savagely into his horse's sides. He rode at a dead run for about a mile before his sanity returned. It wouldn't do to go charging into camp at a run like this. No matter what had happened, it wouldn't do to act like a fool.

He slowed his horse to a relatively silent walk. It was full dark now, but he rode from memory directly toward the gulch in which the others were camped.

He was puzzled at himself. Why did fury leap so much higher at the thought of Hawken hurting Lacy than it did at the thought of Hawken hurting Rufe or Johnny? He didn't know. Perhaps it was just that Lacy was a girl, and more in need of protection.

While yet a quarter of a mile from camp, he dismounted and tied his horse to a clump of brush just at the edge of the hillside. Slipping his rifle from the saddle boot, he advanced on foot, moving as quietly and slowly as a stalking panther.

His thoughts went on unchecked. He had no doubt now that Hawken had fired the shot in camp. Somehow Hawken had gotten his hands on a gun—or he'd tried and been shot by one of the others. Clyde hoped Hawken had been shot. He suspected that Hawken was a worse threat to the safety of the party than the Utes.

He realized that he could turn back, tonight, while there was still time. Carrie would probably get over it eventually. She'd have to. It was time she forgot the war and learned to live with life as it now was. It was time she stopped dreaming of the past and a way of life that was now gone forever.

But he shook his head stubbornly, remembering the way Carrie had looked during the few days before he had left. He couldn't give up. Not yet. Besides, all the others, with the possible exception of Lacy, would want to go on, too.

Ahead of him the tree-choked gulch loomed up, dark and forbidding. Clyde stopped and listened intently, but he heard nothing.

His heart thumped in his chest. Resisting the terrible temptation to go charging into camp immediately, he turned left and began to climb. If Hawken were armed, he would be watching for him to arrive from below or from this side. He would be unprepared for Clyde's arrival from above. Besides, to go in from the western side would put Clyde against the western sky, in which a remnant of light remained, silhouetting him and making him an excellent target.

Careful to make no sound, Clyde climbed steadily for twenty minutes. Then he stopped and listened again.

His heart seemed to plummet into his stomach at what he heard, and his breathing stopped. He felt chills run along his spine. Ahead of him and a little to his right, a horse was stamping and moving about, indicating that he was tied. Clyde listened intently for a moment more, fighting the almost overpowering impulse that seized him to run down the hill into camp. Then, knowing this had to be done first, he crept silently toward the sounds.

It was a horse all right. The horse was tied to a tree, and wore no saddle. A worn, folded blanket lay over his back instead. Clyde waited for a minute more, listening to make sure that his horse was the only one. Then he turned down the gulch, moving with all the haste he could manage, but considering also the need for utter silence.

That single shot had been heard by someone other than Clyde himself. And now, between himself and the camp, an Indian was stalking along silently.

For an instant, panic ran unchecked through Clyde. Perhaps the warrior was already standing at the edge of camp, looking into it. Perhaps he was already drawing back his bow to send an arrow into one of the unsuspecting whites.

Again the compulsion to charge headlong down the hill came over Clyde. He resisted it, and drew back the hammer of his rifle. He had to get the Indian silently, if possible. No telling how many more were camped within sound of a rifle shot.

A slight breeze stirred, blowing up the gulch. Clyde's nose caught the smell of campfire smoke, though it seemed to be more the smell of a dead fire than a live one. Damn it, what was the matter with them down there? Couldn't they use their heads at all? That smoke smell was like a beacon, guiding the stalking Indian straight to them. And if the fire were still burning, the Indian could pick off every damned one of them without even showing himself.

Suddenly, then, Clyde's nose caught another smell, one he recognized instantly. It was the rank, rancid smell of an Indian, compounded of campfire smoke absorbed in buckskin, and long, braided hair. It was the smell of animal blood, stale grease and sweat. It was a wild smell that made the hair stir on the back of Clyde's neck. He could feel his muscles bunch in his body. He halted, and checked the direction of the wind. The smell faded, and returned again, stronger than before. Clyde knew suddenly that he could be no more than fifteen or twenty feet from the brave or the smell would not have been so strong.

It was pitch black here in the grove. No starlight

filtered through the leafy covering overhead.

Clyde made his breathing slow and quiet. He moved not a muscle as he stood listening. He could feel the flesh crawl along his spine.

He didn't know how long he stood, but at last his patience was rewarded. He heard the stealthy movement of the Indian ahead of him. Oddly, it was no sound he could identify; it seemed to be sensed rather than distinctly heard. Perhaps it was the sibilant murmur of clothing, or the light sound of breathing. But from the closeness of it, he judged the Indian was about ten feet ahead.

Clutching the rifle so tightly that his knuckles ached, he eased forward.

This was, he realized, the fateful moment. If his foot stirred a rock, or a twig, the sound was bound to alert the brave, who might either turn and give battle, or fade silently into the brush and disappear. Clyde knew he couldn't let that happen, for if it did there'd be a dozen braves down on them by dawn tomorrow.

Like a shadow, he went on. The Ute was moving slowly. He didn't know Clyde was behind him; he thought he had all night, if he needed it, for the task he'd set himself.

With agonizing slowness, Clyde closed the distance between them. Once he saw the Indian, a blacker shape against a willow turned gold by early frost. And then, from ahead, he dimly caught the sound of Johnny's adolescent voice, followed by another, even fainter, that sounded like a groan.

The camp, then, was fairly close. Soon the Indian would reach the edge of the clearing. And when he did . . .

Clyde stepped up his pace. He caught another, stronger whiff of the Indian smell, and suddenly saw the shadow of the brave in the darkness ahead. He eased the hammer of his rifle down. Then, abandoning caution, he lunged ahead, clubbing the rifle by its barrel and holding it ready over his right shoulder.

The Indian pivoted like a startled cat. Clyde heard the sharp twang of a bowstring. Something tugged at his shoulder of his coat—the arrow, he supposed. Then he was on the Ute, swinging the clubbed rifle. He felt it collide with something soft, and then his charging body struck the Ute and bowled him back.

The brave fought savagely, with never a sound. At close quarters, Clyde's rifle was useless, so he let it slip from his hands.

Together, grappling, they plunged into a bush with a crash. The brave's legs locked around Clyde's body.

The bow snapped as their combined weight rolled on it, and the quiver of arrows tore loose from the brave's shoulder. A knife slashed through Clyde's coat, nicking the flesh beneath, but was turned from its lethal path by a quick roll of his body. He grappled, trying with both hands for the knife hand of the Ute. The palm of one hand encountered the razor-sharp blade, but Clyde didn't even feel the cut.

With the Indian's smell strong in his nostrils, he secured a grip on the wrist of the hand that held the knife. He got both hands upon it, and twisted with all his strength.

The Ute uttered a low grunt of pain, but he held onto the knife. Arching his body violently, he flung Clyde aside, and then followed, leaping atop him. The twist broke the hold of one of Clyde's hands. The strength of the wiry warrior was astonishing.

Grappling again desperately, Clyde secured another two-handed hold on the knife wrist of the Ute. And this time he nearly broke the brave's arm with the violent suddenness of his wrench. The knife slipped away, lost in the brush through which they rolled.

Clyde released his hold on the Indian's arm. Grappling for the throat, his hands encountered the long, greasy braids of hair. His head struck a rock. The Indian's hands clawed for his throat and closed upon it. Clyde reared back, breaking the hold. Then he looped one of the waist-long braids around the Indian's throat and tightened it savagely, bringing up a thrashing knee into the groin of the Ute.

It was like wrestling a greased pig. The Indian

bucked and twisted and rolled beneath him. But the braid tightened inexorably, as Clyde straddled the wiry brave's chest. Slowly the strength of the Indian ebbed. His struggles grew weaker, and his chest heaved with its efforts to draw life into his lungs.

A primeval savagery rose in Clyde's brain. Without loosening the noose from the brave's throat, he began to bang the Indian's head against the rocky ground, as though the brave were something vile that had to be pounded and smashed and completely destroyed. It seemed an eternity before the Ute went limp, and when he did, Clyde still continued to beat his head against the ground.

He was slow to come out of the fury that had possessed him. When he did, he rose to his feet, sobbing for breath, trembling.

Going to hands and knees, he groped up the slope for his rifle and after a few frantic moments, recovered it. Feeling his way, he returned to the Ute.

There was no hesitation in him as he stood over the Ute. Deliberately he brought his rifle butt down in a smashing, savage blow against the Indian's skull. The sound of it was sodden and dull.

Without regret, he stepped away and laid the rifle down. The Ute had not been dead, but he was now.

Kneeling, Clyde seized the Indian's wrist and felt for a pulse. There was none. He put his hands on the Indian's chest. Neither was there movement there.

Sweating, he rose again and recovered his rifle. For an instant he stood listening. He heard the run of Johnny's voice in camp down the slope from him. Hell, they hadn't even heard the struggle. The wind, blowing up the gulch, must have kept the sound of it away from them. He had to grin at that. He waited long enough for his knees to steady and for his breathing to quiet. Then he moved cautiously down the hill toward camp.

As he moved toward the nearly silent camp, an unpleasant foreboding came over Clyde. It was an odd feeling, and one he didn't like.

He knew that it was caused in part by his self-revulsion over what he had done. Until tonight, he had never killed a human being, and had never expected to. Yet he was aware that he'd had no choice tonight. If he'd let the Indian live, he would have been committing suicide. He would have been guilty of killing, indirectly, all those who were with him. By dawn, the Indian would have brought a score of braves against the little party of whites.

Clyde had been forced by circumstances into what he'd done. And he was aware that sympathy for the dead Indian was misplaced. The Utes had wantonly butchered the peaceful inhabitants of the White River Indian Agency. Even now they were battling the troops from Fort Steele. If they could, they'd wipe them out. The sooner he put the incident out of his mind the better. The thing to do now was find out what had prompted the shot in camp—and who, if anyone, had been hurt by it.

Time enough later to return and dispose of the Indian's body. They couldn't afford to leave it above ground, for tomorrow it would draw vultures and the vultures would lead the Indian's comrades straight to this spot. So he slipped along quietly, trying to still the uneasy turmoil of his mind.

At last he stood on the edge of camp, trying to penetrate the inky blackness with his eyes.

Again the tension of impending combat gripped him. Whatever he faced in camp was as deadly as what he had faced only moments before. He was sure of that.

CHAPTER 9

BY THE almost nonexistent light of the stars, Clyde picked out, one by one, the shapes of those in camp.

Lacy sat on a log, her head raised in an attitude of intent listening. Near her was a lumped shape on the ground that might be either Rufe or Johnny, or merely a huge rock. Another form paced restlessly back and forth, and Clyde recognized this one as Johnny. Hawken was visible nowhere.

The dead fire smell was stronger here. And there was a feel of trouble in the air, because of Lacy's attitude of listening, or because of Johnny's nervousness—or because of Hawken's absence.

Concealed well by brush, Clyde spoke suddenly, "Who fired that shot?"

His voice broke unexpectedly over the clearing. Lacy jumped violently. Johnny halted and swung around, his stance one of startled fright.

Lacy cried sharply, "Clyde! Look out! He's got a gun!"

"Then he'd better use it. Or throw it down. Because if he doesn't, I'm going to kill him."

He had not yet moved, knowing that until he did he was invisible to the others. His eyes searched the clearing anxiously.

He caught movement on the far side of it as Hawken came from the shadows. Hawken's voice blustered, "What about *your* shot? Maybe the Injuns figured that last shot was fired by one of their own, hunting. But they'll sure as hell investigate a second shot, particularly at night."

Clyde said coldly, "They investigated the first one. There's a dead Indian up on the slope behind me."

Hawken's voice was surly. "Then there's probably more. Hell, man, you can't take this gun away from me." His voice became wheedling. "I got a right to protect myself."

Clyde said evenly, "You've got no rights at all. Now throw down that gun before I blow it out of your hands."

"You can't see me no better than I can you."

"Want to bet your life on it?"

Hawken was silent. Slowly, furtively, he brought the rifle to his shoulder and swung the muzzle back and forth. The swing told Clyde that Hawken couldn't see him at all, and knew his general direction only by the sound of his voice.

An unaccustomed restlessness rode in Clyde. The venture was doomed if he fired at Hawken, or if Hawken fired at him. The dead Indian had certainly not been alone, and another shot would bring others. But the venture was also doomed if he let Hawken intimidate him, or run a bluff.

Actually, he had no intention of forcing Hawken to travel through the reservation unarmed. That would be the rankest kind of stupidity. But Hawken had to be shown that Clyde couldn't be intimidated. He had to get that straight in his mind right now.

Clyde chuckled contemptuously. "What're you going to shoot at, Hawken? You think you've got any chance of hitting me, waving your gunbarrel like that?"

"You can't see me no better than I can you."

"Can't I? How do you suppose I knew you were waving your gunbarrel if I can't see you? You think I heard it?"

Hawken lowered the rifle. Clyde said softly, "That's right. Lower your gun. You can't see either me or your sights so there ain't a hell of a lot of sense in holding it to your shoulder."

He waited for a moment more. Then his voice cut through the darkness like the flick of a whip. "Drop it, you son of a bitch! This is the last time I'm going to tell you."

Hawken dropped the gun. Clyde said, "Now step away from it."

Hawken did.

Clyde said, "Johnny, go pick it up." Then he stepped out into the clearing. He said, "All right.

What the hell was that shot for? Didn't I tell you . . ."

Lacy got up and ran to him. For an instant he thought she would fling herself into his arms, but she stopped short without even touching him.

Sensing the turbulence in her, he started to reach for her, then dropped his hands. If he touched her now, she'd go to pieces.

She spoke with forced calmness that betrayed her agitation. "Clyde, Rufe is hurt. Hawken's bullet went through his shoulder."

Shock touched Clyde instantly. "Is he bad?" He realized that his own voice contained the same suppressed calmness which Lacy's had.

"The bullet missed the bone, and it went clear through. But he can't travel, Clyde."

"He's got to travel." Clyde's voice sounded harsh and unsympathetic, even to his own ears. He crossed to the lumped shape on the ground, knelt and touched Rufe's leg gently. "You awake, Rufe?"

"Sure, Clyde. I'm all right."

"How do you feel?"

"Like in the war, only it ain't my head that hurts this time. It's my shoulder."

"All right. Go to sleep if you can." He got up stiffly and said to no one in particular, "I had to leave my horse, but I've got a bottle of whisky in the saddlebags. I'll get it. Hawken, you and

Johnny come with me. We've got to get that damned Indian under the ground."

Johnny's voice shook. "How we goin' to dig?"

"With knives, with your fingers if you have to. Come on." He hesitated for the barest instant, then added, "Johnny, leave your gun behind. Lacy, if Hawken comes back to camp before I do, shoot him."

He led out, then, and Lacy returned to sit with Rufe, keeping her rifle beside her.

When Clyde reached the Indian's body, he stopped and told them where to dig. The ground was soft and there were rocks nearby which they could pile on the grave to keep wolves from disturbing the body. Clyde continued up the hill until he reached the Indian's horse. He took the bridle and blanket off and turned it loose. Then, swinging downslope, he walked steadily until he came to the place where he'd left his own horse.

Mounting, he returned to Johnny and Hawken. He called out softly as he approached.

They had a grave large enough for the Indian's body begun. Clyde dismounted and searched around until he found the Indian's broken bow, his quiver of arrows and his knife. By the time he had found them, the grave was finished.

He tossed the Indian's weapons and his bridle and blanket into the grave. Johnny hung back, not wanting to touch the body, hut Hawken didn't seem to mind. He seized it by the feet, dragged it over and dumped it into the grave. He began to shove dirt into it with his feet. Johnny helped him. Clyde dismounted and carried rocks to the grave with which to cover it.

He worried a little about the Indian's horse, but he knew he'd done the only thing he could. If he'd killed the horse, the buzzards would have drawn the Indians here tomorrow. If he'd kept the horse, the animal would have been living proof of the killing. No, he'd done the only thing he could, but he couldn't help worrying about it. His only chance was that the horse, instead of returning to the Indian's latest campsite, would return to some more permanent place—perhaps the village from which he had been originally taken—or that the horse would not return at all. Otherwise, the Indians would, in the morning, simply track the horse back here.

He shrugged, straightening from his task. "All right. Let's get back to camp."

He led his horse back downhill, while Hawken and Johnny followed silently behind. When he reached the camp, he unsaddled and picketed his horse with the others. Then he returned, got the flat bottle of whisky from his saddlebags, and took it to Rufe. "This will help you sleep, Rufe." His voice was gentle. He raised Rufe's head and held the uncorked bottle to his lips. Rufe drank liberally, and then began to cough. Clyde corked the bottle and returned it to his saddlebags.

Turning, he asked Hawken, "How are your hands?"

"Painful as hell. More'n likely they'll keep me awake all night. But if I had a snort or two of that . . ."

"That's for Rufe. He'll need all of it and more before we're through."

He sat down and rested his back against his saddle. He couldn't trust Hawken to stand guard, and he didn't want to ask Lacy. She'd have her hands full taking care of Rufe. Guarding camp was going to have to be up to Johnny Sauls and himself. Johnny, young as he was, might have trouble staying awake on the second watch. So Clyde said, "Johnny, you take the first watch. Wake me up at midnight."

"How'm I goin' to know . . ."

Clyde stifled his impatience. "Guess at it, Johnny."

Lacy sat silently beside Rufe, hunched a little either against the cold, or automatically, because of fear. Clyde closed his eyes and tried to relax. But he kept imagining that he smelled the Indian, and he kept remembering the sound his gun butt had made, striking the Indian's skull.

He thought of Carrie, and wondered briefly if she had realized what the consequences of sending him and the others into the reservation might be. How many times would he kill before he emerged on the other side? And how many more of their party would be hurt, or killed?

He stared up at the stars. A wind stirred, rustling the leaves of the trees in the gulch, and whispered through the high sagebrush and serviceberry brush. It was a chill wind, straight out of the north, moisture-laden and damp. Their chances would be sharply reduced if it snowed.

Lacy spoke a few words softly to Rufe. Then she left him and came to sit beside Clyde, blanket-wrapped and seeming childlike, and helpless because she was. Johnny had taken up his vigil by the trunk of a huge willow at the edge of the clearing.

Lacy's voice was a whisper. "Clyde, we just can't go on. We've got to turn back."

He didn't answer.

"Clyde, did you hear me?"

"I heard you. But we're not going back."

"You can't mean that! Rufe's hurt. He may die if we don't get him to a doctor."

Clyde said impatiently, "We're three days from home. We're three days from accomplishing what we set out to do. It won't make any different to Rufe whether he's riding east or west. He's got three days of riding any way you look at it."

"Is there a doctor for him on the other side of the reservation?"

"He won't need one."

"No. It's very possible that he won't."

"What the hell do you mean by that?"

"I mean he may be dead. We may all be dead." There was a touch of anger in her voice.

He said stiffly, "Go to sleep, Lacy. Tomorrow we start gathering cattle. Three days from now we'll be in Utah with close to a thousand head. Know how much money that is? It's thirty thousand dollars."

She did not reply immediately. When she did, her voice was resigned, "All right, Clyde."

For some reason he felt guilty, and because he did, he said, "Damn it, Lacy, nobody asked you to come."

"I know." There was only humility in her voice, but it seemed to Clyde that it was an accusation. He raised his voice and called to the others. "Lacy doesn't want to go on. She thinks it may be dangerous for Rufe. So I'm going to put it up to all of you. Whichever way you vote will decide what we're going to do. I'm damned if I'm going to drag you all into this against your will."

There was silence in the clearing. Clyde could feel Lacy's closeness, and though she was two or three feet away, it seemed almost as though he could feel her warmth. The tiny stream made a rushing, pleasant sound, and the wind sighed softly through the brush and through the golden leaves on the trees.

Clyde said, "Johnny?"

Jonnny's voice was touched with bravado, but

it broke once as he spoke. “I vote to go on. We’ve come too far. . . .”

“Rufe?” asked Clyde.

Rufe’s voice was weak, and twisted with pain. “We got to go on, Clyde. We can’t go back now.”

“Hawken?”

Hawken chuckled softly. “What you askin’ me for? You already got two votes for goin’ on. Yours will make three. That settles it, don’t it?”

Clyde said harshly, “Maybe it does. But I want to hear from you anyhow.”

Again Hawken chuckled. “Why? You tryin’ to ease your conscience? Is that it? You tryin’ to clear yourself for whatever happens before we’re through?”

Clyde clenched his fists. Was that really what he was trying to do? Or was he trying to justify himself with Lacy? This wasn’t a free election at all. The people here, with the exception of Hawken, were too closely bound to each other to ever be wholly free. He realized that if they had been truly free, both Johnny and Rufe would have voted with Lacy to go back. They were going on only because of loyalty to himself and obligation to Carrie.

He said wearily, “Never mind, Hawken. I don’t give a damn what you want anyway.”

“Wait a minute. I didn’t say I wouldn’t vote. Hell, I vote to go on. I came of my own free will; I stand to gain six thousand dollars for three days work, don't I? I'd be a fool to quit." He was silent for a moment, and then he began to laugh. "I might wind up with a hell of a lot more than I bargained for anyway. I might wind up with the whole damn herd, and Lacy to boot."

Clyde said savagely, "You might wind up with a bullet in your guts, too, if you don't keep that big mouth of yours shut."

Hawken chuckled defiantly.

Lacy got up and went over where Rufe lay. She lay down, pillowed her head on the saddle, and arranged her blankets.

Silence fell over the clearing, broken only by the night noises of the wind, the stream, the occasional outbreak of howling from the wolves or barking from the coyotes.

Clyde slept, and waked, and slept again. Somewhere near midnight, Johnny awakened him by shaking him gently. Clyde was cold clear to his bones. Without unwrapping his blanket from around his body, he got up. Johnny said, "I ain't seen nothin', Clyde, or heard anythin' either."

"All right, Johnny. Now get some sleep."

He walked up the slope to westward and found a rock to sit on. There was a crescent moon in the sky now, and by its light he could see the little clearing in which the others were sleeping below him. Johnny's and Rufe's, Hawken's and Lacy's shapes were vague and indistinct, but visible from where he sat. So was the reach of valley visible, and the moon made a white path of reflection on a quiet stretch of the river.

It may have been weariness, or cold, or a combination of the two, but a bleak feeling of foreboding came over him as he sat staring down at the camp.

The others seemed, now that they were endangered, closer and more precious to him than they had before. Rufe, for all his vagueness, was an old and trusted friend. Johnny was like a younger brother. And Lacy . . .

He shook his head savagely. But his thoughts went on.

The venture had not seemed nearly as impossible back in Indian Creek as it now did. Now it seemed like the rankest kind of folly. He thought of the two whites they'd met coming out yesterday. Even these men, who knew the Utes as individuals, who had raced their horses against those of the Utes and collected wagers from them, had sense enough to get the hell out of the reservation.

And gathering cattle—good God, a man couldn't even try to stay under cover while he rode gathering cattle. Every one of the party, even Lacy, would have to ride through this valley in plain daylight, fair game for every Indian that passed through.

Then he thought of Carrie. The trip from Georgia to Colorado must have seemed impossible to her. Indeed, it had been an incredible undertaking. But with perseverance, dogged refusal to give up, Carrie had brought it off. Clyde could do the same with this.

The night wore on, and dawn came at last. Clyde watched the sky in the east slowly begin to turn gray. He knew he ought to move, to wake the others and get started, yet an odd reluctance possessed him. He looked with unconcealed longing toward the plateau they had crossed yesterday. A bunch of elk came out of the timber half a mile down the valley and walked toward the river. They disappeared into the willows and tall brush that lined its banks.

Suddenly Clyde flung aside his blanket and got up. He thrashed his chest with his arms a few moments to warm himself. Then, picking up his blanket, he walked down the slope toward camp.

CHAPTER 10

CLYDE roused Hawken by stirring him roughly with his boot. Johnny was next, but Clyde awakened him gently. He let Rufe sleep, noticing that Rufe's face was flushed with fever.

Turning toward Lacy, he looked down for a moment at her black, silky hair, so raggedly cropped now. The lines of her face were soft and relaxed. When she opened her eyes, they were soft too. Her lips were loose and slightly parted. Because he suddenly felt an urge to kneel and kiss her, he made his voice unnecessarily harsh. "Going to sleep all day?"

She got up at once and walked toward the stream. Hawken started to follow, but Clyde called curtly, "Come back here, damn you!"

Hawken grinned at him insolently. Clyde turned away, scowling.

They ate sparingly of cold, cooked meat from Lacy's supply, and drank water from the stream. Then they started out.

Lacy rigged a sling for Rufe's arm, and Clyde helped him onto his horse. He gave Rufe the revolver he'd taken off Hawken yesterday. He carried Hawken's rifle to him, saying "That's for Indians. I never intended to make you ride unarmed."

Hawken growled, "Nobody told me that."

"Just remember the rifle's for Indians. Try to use it on me and I'll have what I've been looking for—an excuse to kill you. Go on, lead out."

He fell in immediately behind Hawken. Rufe followed him, with Lacy next. Johnny brought up the rear.

As they rode down into the valley, Clyde said, "Lacy, you and Rufe stay in the valley after we begin to gather. I'll ride the south slope because that's the direction the Indians' reinforcements will come from if they come. Hawken, you and Johnny ride the north slope. We ought to cover fifteen miles today, if we're lucky. Keep a lookout for cattle, but don't tie into any spooky or ringy ones. There's plenty without picking that kind up. And most of all, keep your eyes peeled for Indians. All the cattle in the world won't do us any good if we let them surprise us."

There was a light covering of frost on the grass in the valley. Clyde spent the first hour scanning the slopes to north and south with extreme care. He didn't look for horses or mounted men because he was sure he wouldn't see any. He looked instead for the signs that Indians watch, a bird flying up from a tree, a bunch of frightened deer bounding away, a coyote slinking covertly from brush clump to brush clump. He saw nothing.

The sun came up and warmed his back, but it did not ease the nagging uneasiness that had begun to trouble him. He almost had the feeling that he was being watched.

Trying to rationalize it, he glanced over his shoulder at the others. Lacy was silent this morning, almost moody. She avoided meeting his glance. Rufe's face was tight with pain. Johnny was just plain scared. He glanced automatically at the south slope behind them. He saw a magpie raise from the timber as though startled, and fly away. He studied the spot, but saw nothing further.

Not long afterward, he sighted cattle, a small bunch filing in toward water from the northern slope.

He dispatched Johnny and Hawken to ride that slope, telling Hawken to ride near the top, Johnny to ride halfway down. Hawken was to push whatever he found downslope to Johnny, and Johnny was to bring them on to the bottom, together with whatever he had gathered himself.

Clyde watched the pair ride away. Johnny's face was white, but his lips were firm with determination. Hawken seemed to have forgotten everything but the job at hand, and Clyde knew he would do it well. Hawken was smart enough to realize that the more conscientiously he worked, the larger his share would be.

He swung around and looked at Rufe. Rufe's face was still flushed with fever and there was a whiteness around his mouth that didn't look good. Rufe's eyes were tortured and he held himself awkwardly in his saddle as though trying to ease the pain the horse's jolting caused. Clyde said, "Take half an hour to lie down Rufe. It'll take them that long to get up on the slope and get started."

Rufe grinned weakly and shook his head. "I might not be able to get mounted alone, Clyde, and Lacy's not strong enough to boost me up. No. I'll be all right."

Clyde glanced briefly at Lacy, but she refused to meet his eyes. So he rode off across the river and began to climb the southern slope.

His glance swung east, and again he studied the slope from which the magpie had risen. The feeling that he was being watched continued to trouble him.

Could the Indian last night have had others with him? Could it be the Indian's comrades up there now on the slope? He doubted it. It wasn't the Indians' way to lie and spy on a man, unless they were badly outnumbered. Even then, Clyde doubted if they'd have stayed back and watched. They'd have headed out to gather reinforcements. The magpie might have been startled by an animal, but he doubted it.

Now, looking across the valley, he could see Hawken and Johnny climbing steadily on the other side. Johnny was about ten yards behind the older man.

Nervously Clyde scanned the ridge top above Hawken. There probably wouldn't be much traffic through the valley, but it would be a miracle if they didn't run afoul of at least one or two parties of Utes. The file of cattle he had first spotted crossed the valley below him and stopped at the edge of the stream. There were eight in the bunch, and three small calves. Then his attention was attracted by a bunch on the hillside ahead of him. He got above them and began to haze them down toward the floor of the valley.

It was encouraging the way they immediately turned toward the valley floor when they sighted him. It was going to make things much easier if each bunch didn't have to be driven all the way to the bottom. But he followed along, just in case, until they reached the river.

Lacy and Rufe rode slowly along in the valley now, gathering up whatever there was before them.

At noon, Clyde waved Johnny and Hawken in, and rode down himself. Lacy and Rufe now had nearly forty head before them.

By the time Clyde arrived, Johnny had already

helped Rufe from his saddle. Rufe, lying down, was sweating, and his face was gray. Clyde went over and put a hand on Rufe's damp forehead. When he looked up at Lacy, he was smiling. "His fever's broken."

He unbuttoned Rufe's shirt and looked at the bandage. It was soaked with blood.

He made Rufe comfortable by putting a saddle under his head. He sat down, then, and helped himself to a piece of the cold meat Lacy had laid out. In the open valley before him, the cattle spread out and began to graze.

They had halted in the shade of the willows lining the creek, and now, suddenly, Clyde was glad they had. His glance lifted to the ridge to northward, and he saw a small file of horsemen top it and start down through the timber.

They were almost three miles west, and their course would bring them out in the valley at least twice that distance away. The chances that they'd spot Clyde and his companions were slim unless their attention was drawn by movement. Clyde said sharply, "Don't move, anyone." He pointed, and all eyes turned toward the file of Indians. Clyde said, "That must be their crossing. We're going to have to be damned careful from here on."

He finished eating. He was getting tired of the cold meat, but he made no complaint. They had to use it up, before they started on their other supplies. The deer meat wouldn't keep very long.

The file of Indians had now disappeared. Clyde rose, stretching. His glance kept straying eastward along the way they had come. Suddenly he said, "Stay here until I get back. I'm going to scout around."

He saddled up quickly, ignoring the question in the eyes of the others. He rode out, staying in the willows until he found a spot where he could leave them without being exposed to the timbered hillside toward which he was indirectly heading.

Hidden by the timber, he urged his horse along at a brisk pace, climbing steadily; twenty minutes after leaving camp he reached the crest of the ridge.

Here he dismounted. He tied his horse at the foot of a giant spruce, and fighting his way in to the trunk of the tree, began to climb. The heavy branches clawed at his clothes, but otherwise, climbing was easy because of the closely set branches of the tree. After a few moments he reached the top.

From here, the whole country seemed to be spread before him like a map. He gave a brief glance to the land to the west before he concentrated his gaze on the part of the hillside that lay above the stretch of valley they had covered this morning. He studied it for a long time, seeing nothing. Then, unexpectedly, about a mile away he saw a glint of sun on something bright.

He marked the spot carefully in his mind, using for landmarks a huge, lightning-split pine and an outcropping of reddish rock. Then he climbed carefully down the tree.

Mounting quickly, he set out, planning his course so that he would come in above the spot he sought and thus be able to keep in sight the landmarks he had chosen. He'd been right this morning. They had been watched.

Tension built up in him as he rode. He knew he ought to go back and get Hawken, but he didn't. Hawken, in a scrape, might be more dangerous than whatever they faced. Clyde had no illusions about the man. Hawken would never be satisfied with a one-sixth share if he thought he could get more—and the only way he'd ever get more was by killing Clyde.

A quarter-mile from the place he had spotted the reflection, Clyde dismounted again and tied his horse. Then, silently, he moved on down the slope afoot. He heard the soft run of talk long before he brought the men in sight. They spoke English, and their voices had a certain familiar ring to them.

Clyde halted for a moment, listening, but unable to make out any of their words. He knew them now. Whitey Blake and Hal Arnold. The two who had raced their horses against the Utes.

He knew what had happened, too. Not believing that Clyde and his companions had indeed been heading for Utah, they'd tagged along to see what was really in the wind. Now, besides Hawken, Clyde would have them to worry about. Above all, he'd have to see that Hawken did not join forces with them.

He slipped through the heavy timber as silently as an Indian until he brought their camp into sight. Blake sat on the ground, smoking a pipe. Arnold stood with his back to the lightning-split pine, a pair of binoculars in his hand.

Clyde stepped from behind a screen of brush. Both the men whirled, startled. Clyde said, "I thought someone was following us."

Blake grinned. "We got curious. Didn't seem logical that people would pick this route to go to Utah, knowin' the Utes were kickin' up a fuss. We figured there was another reason. An' there was, sure as hell."

Clyde said, "So?"

Blake's eyes twinkled, but Clyde had the feeling that there was little real humor in the man. "So we like to make a dollar just as well as the next man. With our business shot because the damn government can't get along with the Utes—well, maybe the government owes us a little something."

Clyde said flatly, "But I don't."

Blake shrugged expressively. "Maybe not. We'll wait an' see. You could use us, mister. We just might mean the difference between gettin' through with those cattle and gettin' killed tryin'."

A feeling of helplessness rose in Clyde. He tried not to let it show. He said, "Stay clear of us. I'm edgy, here in Indian country. Anybody snooping around our camp is more likely than not to wind up dead."

Blake grinned insolently. "Sounded like somebody in your camp got hurt last night. Accident?"

Clyde nodded, certain the other would not believe him.

"You're lucky that shot didn't bring a dozen Utes down on you."

Clyde shrugged. "It did bring one. He's dead."

Something close to respect shone briefly in Blake's eyes. He said, perhaps too casually, "That big man with you—he the one that had the accident with the gun?"

Clyde stared at him without answering.

Blake grunted, "Thought so. I noticed yestiddy that he didn't have no guns. Could be he ain't really one of you. He didn't look like he belonged."

Clyde said, "He's one of us. But you aren't. Just stay clear. Understand?"

Blake's eyes turned briefly hard. "That ain't very neighborly, mister. There's enough here for everybody—if nobody gets greedy. There's a thousand cattle between here and the agency. They're good cattle, worth thirty or forty dollars a head. We're goin' to get our share, mister, whether you like it or not. If you was smart you'd take us along with you. We could do our share of the work, an' our share of the fightin' when it comes. With us, you got a chance. Without us, you're cooked. Think it over."

Clyde shook his head stubbornly. If it hadn't been for Hawken, he'd probably have agreed. But he knew these two would come as a godsend to Hawken. All Hawken would have to do was team up with them, and instead of a sixth, he'd get a third.

He backed cautiously into the brush without taking his eyes off either of them. Only when he had placed a thick screen of brush between the pair and himself, did he turn and walk away. He reached his horse, mounted and headed directly back toward the place he had left the others.

Anger stirred in the back of his mind, mounting with every passing minute. He was alone against Hawken, against these two, against the whole Ute nation. Rufe, wounded, would be no help. Johnny was already badly scared; he might panic when the time for fighting came. And Lacy was a girl.

He knew what to expect of Blake and Arnold. They'd follow along, staying hidden, letting Clyde and his companions take the brunt of fighting through the valley. Then, when the job was done, the cattle gathered, they'd move in.

With a sudden burst of anger, Clyde spurred his horse. The startled animal broke into a hard gallop.

Short of the camp, Clyde reined him in, and approached at a walk. He’d have to keep his head. He and the others were in the worst danger they had ever been in their lives. It would take clear thinking and constant vigilance, or they wouldn’t get out alive.

CHAPTER 11

HE FOUND the others much as he had left them. As he rode into camp, all except Rufe looked up at him questioningly.

Johnny asked, “See anything, Clyde?”

Clyde shook his head. He could keep Hawken in ignorance of Blake and Arnold for a time, and intended to as long as possible. Furthermore, he intended to keep Hawken in camp even after he learned of the others’ presence. The longer he was able to keep them separated, the better chance he’d have. Arnold and Blake would not attack as long as Hawken was with Clyde’s party. But if Hawken changed sides, an attack would be inevitable, if not at once then later, when most of the cattle had been secured.

It angered Clyde to realize that Hawken had become the key to success, that whichever side had him would inevitably get the cattle.

He said, “Hawken, you ride in the valley this afternoon. Help Lacy keep the cattle bunched and moving. Rufe’s too sick to work.” He looked at Johnny, “Can you manage the north slope alone?”

"Sure, Clyde." But there was little conviction in Johnny's tone.

Lacy broke in, "Clyde, this is suicide. We can't possibly ride the length of this valley without running into Indians."

"I don't expect to. What I do expect is that those coming from the north will have their bellies full of fighting for a while. They probably won't bother us unless they think there's a chance to pick one of us off without much trouble. At the first sign of Indians, I want every one of you to hunt cover and stay perfectly still. If they spot us, I want you all to hightail it down here into the valley. If we're together we can give them a fight."

Clyde mounted. Johnny saddled his own horse and followed suit. Looking down at Lacy, Clyde said, "Let Rufe rest another half an hour. Hawken can help him get mounted."

He rode away, disappearing immediately into the timber that covered the hillside.

The afternoon was an eternity of tormented worry for Clyde. Looking across the valley, he occasionally saw Johnny working busily on the northern slope.

He knew he had no business letting Johnny work over there alone. Suppose another party of Utes came over the ridge? Johnny wasn't equipped to take care of himself against them. And if he didn't happen to spot them soon enough to run . . .

He shook his head. Johnny wouldn't be any better off over here. He should be in the valley with Lacy and Rufe. The only thing was, if Clyde put Hawken on that hillside, Blake and Arnold were sure to try and reach him.

Having done what was the only possible thing he could, Clyde should have been able to stop worrying and accept whatever came. But he couldn't. Johnny and Lacy and Rufe were his responsibilities.

Down in the valley, as the afternoon progressed, the herd of cattle slowly grew until there were almost two hundred head. Rufe jogged along half a mile behind, slumped in his saddle. Lacy and Hawken rode along the valley floor, gathering and holding the herd together. Mostly Lacy stayed behind the herd, while Hawken did the hard riding.

Had Clyde not realized that Hawken was working only for himself, he would have been grateful to him. He was certainly making it easy on Lacy, and he was doing an efficient, thorough job.

Clyde was deeply relieved when the sun dropped to the western horizon and slid behind it. But he was also disturbed by the bank of clouds building up in the north. A storm now could be disastrous.

He picked up a small bunch of cows with calves and rode behind them to the bottom. Looking up toward where Johnny was working, he waved the boy in. Johnny came willingly and at once, his haste betraying the fact that his fear had been considerable all afternoon.

Clyde felt a stir of admiration for the boy. It took courage to ride that slope alone, knowing that at any minute a band of hostiles might come over the ridge. Johnny had admitted to being scared several days before. He had showed it constantly since. Going ahead, even in the face of his fear, showed what stuff he was made of.

Lacy's face was grimed with dust from riding in the drag of the herd. It was pale and drawn as he rode to where she sat her horse beside a quiet stretch of river. She gave him a wan smile. Clyde said gently, pointing, "We'll camp in that little draw. Go on up there and lie down for a while, Lacy. You'll feel better."

"I feel all right, Clyde." Her eyes seemed unusually large tonight, and held an expression that was strange to them, as though she had stopped trying to change the unchangeable and had accepted something she had been unable to accept before.

Rufe came walking his horse toward them, and Johnny crossed the valley at a fast trot, driving three steers before him. He put them into the bunch and came on to swing down wearily beside Clyde. Rufe caught up shortly thereafter. Clyde studied his face with worried concern.

Rufe was weaker tonight; that was obvious. He'd probably lost a lot of blood today. His face was gray, caked with sweat and dust. His eyes were pinched with pain, but he grinned weakly at Clyde. His eyes held more awareness than was usual for him as he said, "We got a good start today, didn't we, Clyde?"

Clyde nodded. "We sure did. You go with Lacy now, and try to get some sleep."

Lacy rode slowly away and Rufe followed. Clyde stared at Hawken, approaching from the bunched herd. He said, "Johnny, you can quit worrying so much about being scared. It took real guts to ride that slope alone all afternoon. Plenty of grown men wouldn't have done it."

Johnny's eyes were grateful. His freckled face broke into a grin. "I still don't know what I'd do if a bunch of 'em came howlin' down on me. Does a man ever get over bein' scared, Clyde?"

"The only man that isn't afraid of danger is one that doesn't think. That doesn't include you."

A little of Johnny's color had returned. His grin was almost cocky.

Hawken rode up. Even disliking the man as he did, Clyde had to admit that Hawken had certainly pulled his weight. He appeared to be tired, and for once had nothing to say. Clyde looked out across the open valley and observed that the cattle were quietly grazing. He said,

"Come on. We'll get out of sight until dusk. Time enough then to bunch the cattle a little."

He led out toward the draw he'd told Lacy would be their camping place.

When he got there, he dismounted and rubbed his horse down with handfuls of dry grass. Johnny followed suit. Then they picketed the horses out at the head of the draw, along with Hawken's and Lacy's. Clyde kept Rufe's horse in camp, letting him graze with the reins dragging.

He laid down on the ground, conscious of the weariness running through him, conscious too that it was not all caused by the physical work he had done today, though that had been considerable. He was worried and edgy, made more so by the presence of Blake and Arnold up there somewhere in the timber, by the knowledge that sooner or later they would get to Hawken no matter how hard he tried to prevent them.

Lacy brought him a couple of pieces of venison and he ate them, washing them down with water from his canteen. Lacy sat down close to him and ate her own meat, not looking at him. Hawken growled with reluctant admiration, "I never seen such a bunch of knot-heads! But I'll be damned if it don't look like you might get away with it."

Clyde said, "We'll get away with it." But he had no real belief in his own statement.

The valley was now cool and gray with dusk. A haze almost like smoke lay over the river. The air was crisp and strong with the odors of spruce and sage, but it had, tonight, an unaccustomed dampness that promised a storm.

He looked across at Johnny. The boy was beat, sprawled out on the ground with his eyes closed. He said, "Johnny, maybe you'd rather take the second watch. Maybe you'd rather get some sleep now."

Johnny spoke without opening his eyes. "Whatever you say, Clyde."

"All right. Let's do it that way." He got up and went to Rufe's horse. He mounted stiffly and rode slowly out into the meadow. He hated to leave Hawken unguarded, but neither did he want to tell any of the others about the presence of Blake and Arnold nearby. Telling them would only frighten them more.

Besides, there wasn't much danger that Hawken would go wandering off alone, as long as he was unaware of the pair's presence.

It was dark enough now so that the ridges on both sides of the valley were visible only as looming shadows, but there was light enough to see the dark shapes of the cattle. Clyde rode around them slowly, pushing them into a compact bunch. Some of them were already lying down. When he had bunched them, he dismounted on a high spot from which he could look down. Unless something frightened them, they should stay quiet all night.

Hawken was still a threat; he still had a gun and he probably intended to use it the first chance he got. So Clyde stayed awake and wary as the hours passed.

For a while he actually hoped Hawken would come out and have a try at him. If he killed Hawken, he'd have a better chance of pulling this off—as far as the danger from Blake and Arnold was concerned anyway. But with Hawken gone, gathering the cattle would be doubly difficult. And in a fight with Indians . . . However he distrusted Hawken, he needed him badly now that Rufe was hurt.

He came suddenly erect with a start as several of the cattle lumbered to their feet and started away. Looking out across the meadow, he thought he saw a figure coming toward him.

He snatched his revolver from its holster. Muffling it against his body, he slowly thumbed back the hammer. The figure came on.

Clyde was about to challenge, when Lacy's voice came out of the dark. "Clyde? Where are you?"

"Over here." Hc holstered his gun and watched the cattle she had disturbed. She should know better than to come out here afoot. She could have stampeded the whole damned bunch. But they were settling down again and no harm was done.

Walking slowly and carefully on the uneven

ground, Lacy climbed the rise to where Clyde was. She stood, breathing fast, a couple of yards away. He asked, "Is something the matter?"

"No. I just wanted to talk. Clyde, I'm scared. Rufe's sleeping like he was dead, and Johnny's exhausted. How much longer . . ."

"A couple of days. I don't know exactly how far away the Indian agency is, but we ought to hit it day after tomorrow at the latest. The day after that will see us outside the reservation on the other side."

"Rufe won't last that long without rest."

"He'll have to, Lacy."

"Do you really think we can make it, Clyde?"

He understood how desperately she needed reassurance. And he couldn't honestly give it to her. If she knew about Blake and Arnold . . . He took a sudden step toward her. "Lacy . . ."

With a choked sob, she went into his arms and buried her face on his chest. Her small body shook violently, whether from fear, or cold, or weeping, he couldn't tell.

He held her quietly for a long time. His hand went to her head and he stroked her close-cropped hair gently. It was like silk under his hand.

He felt a vast tenderness for her. "Lacy, it will be all right," he murmured.

"And afterward?" Her voice was so faint it was barely audible, but it contained a bitterness foreign to Lacy.

"Afterward will be all right too. How could it be anything else?"

Lacy drew back. Her voice sounded angry. "How can you be so blind? Do you think she'll need *you* when she has that money?"

Clyde stiffened. Then he relaxed. She was overwrought, and scared. Her face was a pale blur in the darkness. Suddenly, he wished he could see it clearly.

"Will you kiss me, Clyde?"

The question startled him, and for a moment he didn't move. Then he gripped her shoulders and lowered his head, intending to kiss her forehead. Instead he found her lips.

Her arms went tight around his neck. Her body molded itself against him. Her lips were hot and dry, but very soft.

Something began to pound in Clyde's head. He forgot cattle, Indians, Hawken and the pair of horseracers. He forgot Carrie, forgot everything but Lacy, her warmth, her womanliness, her urgency and need. His arms closed hard around her.

He drew back at last, shaken. He whispered hoarsely, "God help me, Lacy, can a man love two women at the same time?"

"No, Clyde. Only one."

He didn't reply.

She said fiercely, "I've been loyal long enough. I'm going to stop right now. I want you to think about something, Clyde, before it's too late. Could a woman who really loved a man send him away to fight his way through territory swarming with Indians? Could she send Johnny and Rufe with him, knowing they might never come back? Could she love them and do that, for nothing but money?"

He growled, "Don't talk like that." But his mind wasn't on his words or even what she'd said to provide them. His mind was on Lacy, who was so near.

She moved even closer and slipped her arms around his waist. "Clyde, don't talk. Kiss me again."

He seized her again and crushed her to him. After a long while he drew away. "I love you, Lacy. I love you more than I thought was possible."

She took one of his hands, sank to the ground and pulled him down beside her. She began to cry softly.

He drew her to him, confused and disturbed. "What are you crying for?"

Her voice was choked. "I guess I'm crying because I know you don't really mean it, Clyde, and because I want you to mean it so much."

"But I do mean it."

She shook her head. "You're worried, like the rest of us. You're trying to take care of us. I'm here, and you need me. That's all there is to it."

Rising to an elbow, he gripped her shoulders and shook her fiercely. "No. That's not all there is to it! I love Carrie. I guess I always have, ever since I was a kid. But it's not like this. It's never been like this. I know now . . ."

She put her hand on his mouth, silencing him. "Don't say things you can't take back, Clyde."

"Then believe me! Lacy . . . Lacy!" He held her tight against him, his body lying partly upon her.

She stirred beneath him. "Clyde, I *want* to belong to you, Clyde. Tomorrow might be too late. I . . ." Her voice died out.

He kissed her eyes, her tear-wet cheeks, and her eager mouth. The time and place were lost. For a while they knew nothing but each other. The knowing was like a sound in Clyde's ears, a rising crescendo of surf breaking upon a shore, of hurricane wind tearing through a stand of pines. But in the end it was quiet, with Lacy soft and spent in his arms, with a peace between them that could never be damaged again.

The moon was up, and by its silver light he could see her face, relaxed and happy and gently smiling. She whispered softly, "Clyde, I love you. I've loved you ever since I was ten."

"You're not sorry?"

"Sorry? How could I be?"

Clyde lay back and stared at the sky. He could hear the cattle stirring sleepily, the sound of the river, the whisper of the rising wind in the tall grass. A frog croaked, and a night bird swooped down toward the river, hunting.

Suddenly, then, Lacy's safety became the most important thing in the world to him. Lacy had to live! And she couldn't live if anything happened here in the reservation that left her without protection. Gently he drew her to him. She was asleep, and she sighed and snuggled close.

She didn't know how slim their chances were; she didn't know about Blake and Arnold. It was too late to back out now, even if he'd wanted to. He and Lacy, Johnny and Rufe would be witnesses against the pair of horseracers and against Hawken even if they turned the herd over to them—witnesses that would never be allowed to testify.

CHAPTER 12

IT WAS well after midnight before Clyde awakened Lacy. She sighed sleepily. He helped her to her feet and went after the horse. He lifted her to the saddle, then mounted behind her. This way, he circled the herd and rode to the draw where the others were sleeping.

He awakened Johnny and talked to him several minutes to be sure the boy was wide awake. After watching Johnny mount and ride into the valley, he rolled himself in his blankets and laid down not far from where Lacy was. She spoke softly in the darkness. "Good night, Clyde."

"Good night, Lacy."

It seemed to be only a moment, and then Johnny was shaking his shoulder. He opened his eyes and saw the gray of dawn in the sky. Sitting up, he asked, "Everything all right?"

"Uh-huh. Except that it's going to storm."

Clyde realized that the wind was strong, and cold. Clouds filled the sky, low, heavy clouds that moved out of the north with terrifying speed.

He got up, stretching. He rubbed his eyes and stared out across the valley floor at the grazing cattle. They were scattering now, but slowly, and would not yet head for the timbered hillsides.

He started to walk toward Lacy. Something made him glance at Hawken, and what he saw stopped him instantly. Hawken had a leering, knowing look on his face that made Clyde furiously angry.

He turned and said to Johnny, "Wake Lacy and Rufe and let's get started." Then he walked across the open valley to the river, a couple of hundred yards away. As he walked, he scanned the hillsides carefully.

Reaching the river, he stopped and splashed water into his face. Then he lay prone and took a long drink. Running his fingers through his hair, he returned quickly to camp.

Lacy was up. Her soft, dark eyes found his face and clung to it. Hawken said under his breath with mocking emphasis, "Good night, Clyde."

Clyde swung and scowled at him. Hawken, on the point of going after his horse, stopped and dropped his saddle. He yanked the rifle out of the boot. He said, "Come on. Try it."

Clyde said harshly, "Get your horse, or I will try it."

Hawken grinned insolently. But he turned and headed up the hill to get his horse. Johnny followed.

Johnny returned first, riding his own horse, leading Clyde's and Lacy's.

Clyde asked, “Where’s Hawken?”

“Still up there. He said he’d be along in a minute.”

Clyde saddled his horse and mounted. He eyed the gray sky with a frown. Then, turning the horse, he rode up the gulch.

Hawken sat his horse in a small clearing to one side of the gulch. He was watching the far hillside intently. “Somebody over there. It ain’t no Injun, either.”

“You’re crazy.”

Hawken peered at him suspiciously. “What the hell are you up to? You know there’s somebody there. And you know who it is.”

“I don’t know what you’re talking about. I don’t see anything.”

“Neither do I—now. But I ain’t wrong about seein’ someone.” He peered intently at Clyde. “You don’t seem very damned worried about it.”

“I’m not. I think this is one of your goddam tricks.”

Hawken studied him a moment, then turned and rode down the gulch. Clyde followed. He’d have to watch Hawken like a hawk from here on. He’d have to see to it that Hawken didn’t get away by himself.

Hawken rode out into the valley, with Clyde and the others straggling along behind. Johnny began to climb his horse up the ridge to the north. Lacy began to bunch the cattle. Rufe held his horse still at the foot of the ridge, waiting.

Hawken passed the bunched cattle, heading toward the far slope. Clyde suddenly realized that the man intended to investigate what he had seen a few moments before, which was something Clyde could not allow. Savagely, he dug spurs into his horse's sides.

The animal broke into a run. Hawken, hearing the pounding hoofs behind him, glanced around. Then he, too, dug spurs into his horse's sides.

They raced across the valley floor splashed wildly across the river and tore through the willows on the far side. Hawken spurred his horse up the steep slope on the south side of the valley. He reached for the rifle in the boot at his side.

Clyde snatched out his revolver, thumbed back the hammer and raised it to eye level. Hawken got his rifle half out of the boot.

Suddenly his horse stumbled, and went to his knees. Hawken was flung from the saddle and catapulted over the horse's head. His rifle fell to the ground at the horse's side.

Clyde swung down, still short of Hawken's rolling body by fifteen yards. He stood spread-legged on the steep slope, his gun in his hand, waiting for Hawken to rise.

Hawken's face was mottled with rage as he struggled to his feet. His cheek was skinned and bleeding, and his mouth was full of dirt. He spat explosively and snarled, "You son of a bitch!"

Clyde said, "Get back down in the valley and do what you're supposed to do!"

"To hell with you. I'm goin' up that hill an' see who's there." He took a step toward his rifle.

Clyde beat him to it. He snatched up the rifle and flung it away.

Hawken, uphill from him, uttered a sound that was half bellow, half growl. He rushed at Clyde.

For an instant temptation was strong in Clyde to shoot the man. He resisted it with an effort, lowered the gun-hammer and shoved the gun back into its holster. He tried to sidestep Hawken, but the man swerved and charged into him with an impact that shook Clyde's teeth. He felt himself flung backwards down the hill, felt the rocky ground grind his back as he struck, sliding. He somersaulted backward, losing his hat, coming to rest on hands and knees facing uphill.

Hawken had rolled even farther than he and now was below him, scrambling toward him. Clyde stood up, whirled and lashed out with his boot as Hawken came within range. He didn't intend to let Hawken get above him on the slope again if he could help it.

The boot connected with Hawken's forehead, but it did not roll him back. Hawken, on hands and knees, lowered his head almost to the ground and shook it ponderously.

Clyde repeated, "Get back down in the valley before I kick your face in!"

Hawken looked up. His eyes were red, and full of fury. They were like bullets in a gun cylinder, filled with a promise to kill. The slyness was gone from Hawken, and the calculation. Now there was left only primeval fury, and animal rage.

He scrambled toward Clyde. And Clyde kicked again. This time Hawken reared up like a bear whose belly has just been bullet burned. His great paws seized Clyde's foot and twisted.

Clyde was turned half around. Deliberately he fell to his knees, and with the other foot lashed back at Hawken.

It broke the man's hold, smashing into his face. Clyde clawed upward on the slope, turned and rose again.

Hawken was up an instant ahead of him, and now came lunging up the hill. Clyde saw that he would try a different tack than he had the first night he'd come into camp. Hawken intended to fight today in Clyde's way, with fists and knees and feet.

Clyde met Hawken with a looping right hook that missed because Hawken ducked. Then something struck him full in the mouth, something that was like the kick of a horse.

He was flung back, spread-eagled on the slope. He saw Hawken plunge toward him and leap. Frantically, he rolled aside, knowing that if Hawken's knees, with all the man's tremendous weight behind them, landed on him he would be smashed and beaten once and for all.

Nor would Hawken stop with that. He was crazy mad, insane with the lust to kill. There would be no stopping him. He'd beat and tear at Clyde until Clyde was dead.

He eluded the deadly knees, but Hawken's hand went out and caught him by the collar of his duck jacket. He heard it rip, and then he flung himself downhill. For an instant the jacket held. Then it tore noisily, and Clyde was sliding, rolling scrambling downhill, while Hawken charged blindly after him.

He recovered, and rose in time to see Hawken coming at him, this time from above. He stood his ground, trembling with exhaustion. He had to end this. Fighting Hawken took a terrible toll of his strength.

Hawken, sure this time, leaped at him. Unexpectedly, Clyde fell to the ground, directly in Hawken's path.

Too late, the man tried to dive, recover and failed. As his body flew through the air at Clyde, Clyde raised himself to his hands and knees. He caught Hawken's body on his back, and the impact drove a grunt of air from his lungs, nearly drove him back to the ground. With all his strength, he raised his body and reared back.

Hawken, arrested in mid-air by Clyde's body, now rose and catapulted down the slope, arms and legs windmilling. Except for the slope, he would not have traveled more than a few feet at most. But here the slope was steep. As Hawken fell, the slope fell away beneath him. He traveled almost a dozen feet before he struck, head first, against the trunk of a giant pine.

The sound was like that of an ax biting into wood. He crumpled to the ground and lay still at the foot of the tree.

Clyde sank to the ground. He dropped his head between his knees, sucking great, gasping breaths of air into his lungs. He was sweating profusely, and his mouth was puffy and bleeding from both corners.

Hearing a crackling of underbrush above him, he glanced up, expecting to see Hawken's horse or his own moving away. Instead he looked into the grinning, bearded face of Blake. Behind Blake was his partner, Arnold. Both were mounted.

Blake said delightedly, "Man, that was a fight! What was it all about?"

Clyde grunted, "Doesn't concern you."

"Now you're wrong about that. Everything that happens concerns us." His right hand strayed to his shirt pocket and brought out a sack of makings. He rolled a cigarette absently, licked it and stuck it in his mouth. He lighted it and drew smoke into his lungs with obvious pleasure. His eyes were sardonic, mocking. "I thought you said he was one of you."

"I did." Clyde wished he knew whether or not he'd lost his gun in the shuffle. He thought he could feel its weight in the holster, but he couldn't be sure.

Blake glanced over Clyde's shoulder at Hawken. "He looks dead."

"Too tough to kill." Clyde turned his head and eyed Hawken where he lay sprawled against the trees. As he did, he let his glance drop and touch his holster. The gun was still there.

He turned and met Blake's eyes, knowing instantly that neither Blake nor Arnold had any intention of leaving until Hawken revived. Nor was he prepared, right now, to try to force them to leave.

He picked his way downhill to where Hawken lay. He rolled the man over on his back. Hawken's chest rose and fell regularly. Clyde examined his head. There was blood on his scalp, and a sizeable knot had risen there.

He sat down to wait for Hawken to revive, ignoring the two mounted men above him. Discouragement touched him, and then was replaced by anger. He knew he should have it out with this pair now, before things went any further. He also knew he wouldn't. He couldn't kill them with no more provocation than the vague threats they'd made. He couldn't kill them until they'd made an overt move, threatened either his own life or the lives of his companions.

He glanced up at Blake. “You’re wasting your time tagging along behind us.”

Blake shrugged good humoredly. “Maybe. Maybe not. Could be the time would come when you’d trade the whole herd for your neck. Or maybe you’ll all get killed by Indians. You wouldn’t want your work to be wasted, would you?”

Clyde said disgustedly, “Damn vultures!”

Anger sparkled in Blake’s eyes. “That kind of an attitude will get you nothin’. You need us. We need you. There’s plenty here for all of us.”

Clyde didn’t answer.

Blake said threateningly, “You better walk soft, mister. How much good do you think your damned cattle are going to do you if me an’ Hal drop a word to the government that you’ve got them? If you don’t cut us in, that’s exactly what we’re goin’ to do.”

Clyde said, “Go to hell.”

He didn’t look at them again. Hawken was stirring. He uttered a low groan.

Clyde watched him closely, meanwhile trying to figure a way out of the fix they had him in. If he took Arnold and Blake in on the deal, it would make things easier, except that they’d crowd him out. He’d get nothing from the sale of the cattle. Probably he wouldn’t even stay alive.

Nor would it help him to turn them in afterward, as they had threatened to do with him. He was as guilty as they were, regardless of whether or not he shared in the loot. He had begun the theft.

Arnold and Blake, on the other hand, were in the clear so far. They were the only witnesses to the theft. They could turn Clyde and his party in to the government with impunity.

No. He couldn't take them in, and he couldn't fail to take them in. He had only one hope—that the Indians would get Blake and Arnold before they got through the reservation, or that they'd attack his party and give him an excuse to kill them.

Hawken presented still another hazard. He was wily and dangerous, and if he had hated Clyde before, he would hate him doubly now. He would know, upon coming to, that Arnold and Blake were following. It wouldn't take him long to see the possibilities of teaming up with them.

Clyde's thoughts were cut short by Hawken, who opened his eyes and struggled to sit up. He looked blankly at Clyde, then at Whitey Blake and Hal Arnold.

He frowned, and put a hand to his head. "God! My head!" He seemed to remember and looked balefully at Clyde. Then he asked, "What're they doin' here? I thought . . ."

Blake broke in smoothly, "You thought we were headed out of the reservation. We were, but we got curious about you folks. Seemed funny a party like yours would be headin' right smack into the reservation in the middle of an uprising. So we followed to see what was up. Now all we want is to be cut in. What do you say?"

Clyde spoke before Hawken had a chance. "No. Now get the hell out of here."

Blake kept staring at Hawken. He asked, "Is he the boss? Or are you?"

Clyde said, "I am. Come on, Hawken. I'll help you to your horse."

Hawken struggled to his feet, using the pine for support. He growled, "Get away from me, you bastard!"

Clyde turned and climbed the hill alone. He picked up his hat, caught his horse and swung to the saddle. He felt alone and vulnerable. If Hawken took a notion to team up with this pair right now he wouldn't have a chance.

He slid his hand along his thigh until it rested no more than two inches from his gun.

Hawken found his rifle and staggered to his horse. He clung with both hands to the horn as he mounted. Afterward he sat there groggily, his face white and sick.

Clyde felt a touch of hope. Hawken was in no shape to think anything through right now, particularly something as touchy and dangerous as changing sides. He said, "Go ahead, Hawken. I'll follow."

Hawken scowled at him, but he put his horse

down the hill toward the valley. Clyde followed. Blake and Arnold sat their horses, unmoving, and watched.

Clyde followed Hawken all the way to the bottom, where Lacy and Rufe were waiting. He said, “Lacy, do you remember the two we met on the way in here—the horseracers?”

She nodded.

Clyde said, “They’re following us. They want to be cut in, but I turned them down.”

Hawken edged his horse away and rode to the river bank. He dismounted and dunked his head in the river. Clyde said, his voice low so that Rufe wouldn’t hear, “You might as well know what we’re up against. Those two are going to try and move in on us as soon as we get the herd gathered up. They’ll probably try to get Hawken on their side. If they do we won’t have much chance.”

“Clyde, why can’t we leave? Why can’t we give it up?”

He grinned ruefully. “Because I don’t think they’d let us—now. They think I might go to the government. They’re not sure, but if we tried to leave they’d make sure I didn’t.”

“You mean they’d kill us?”

He nodded. “There’d be no risk in it for them. If we were found dead, it would be assumed the Indians had killed us. Nobody would ever bother to look farther than that.”

She gave him a scared little smile.

He said, “Lacy, I’ll get you out of this.”

“I know you will.”

He turned and rode up the hill to begin the morning’s gather. His eyes were full of smoldering anger, and cold determination.

CHAPTER 13

THE WIND increased as the morning progressed, and by noon, tiny, stinging flakes of snow were pelting out of the north.

Dust rose from beneath the hoofs of Clyde's horse. Down in the valley, more dust rose from the hoofs of several hundred cattle. Clyde hadn't tallied them, but he guessed they numbered over three hundred head. Both he and Johnny were finding more today than they had yesterday. Probably most of the herd had been bunched down here close to the Agency.

Noon came, but he didn't stop. He only rode to the bottom, got a couple of chunks of meat from a dusty, weary Lacy and rode back up on the hillside.

The impending storm bothered him tremendously. If it became very cold, or if it snowed much, the Utes up north were likely to weary quickly of fighting and break off the engagement. Which would mean that shortly thereafter, hundreds or even thousands of Ute warriors would be streaming through the valley on the way to the villages in the south.

Ahead, now, he could see a haze of bluish smoke in the distance to westward. The agency buildings and haystacks, he guessed, or what was left of them, still smoldering.

The day passed, without growing colder. The snow abated, but the fact stirred little jubilation in Clyde, for he knew that conditions could easily change overnight. By morning there could be a foot of snow on the ground. And to travel through such deep snow, leaving tracks behind, would be suicide. If it snowed, they'd simply have to hole up until the snow was gone. Or go back.

Now, at nightfall, his mind seemed numb and without ability to feel. His body, sore from the fight with Hawken, weary from the jolting of the day's riding, seemed without life. The debt he owed Carrie seemed obscure and unreal to him now. Carrie herself, and his love for her, seemed far away. He halted his horse and stared blankly across the valley at Johnny, working the north slope.

Looking back east, his eye caught movement near the top of the ridge, and suddenly his body turned cold. For he saw a file of Indians come riding over the crest of the ridge and halt abruptly.

His glance swiveled immediately to Johnny. Johnny was industriously working the side of the ridge, unconscious of the peril behind him. Clyde guessed the Indians had not yet seen Johnny.

Their attention seemed to be focused on the herd in the bottom, on Lacy and Hawken and Rufe, following along behind.

Clyde put his glance back on the Indians, studying them. Obviously, they had just come from the battle. One of them, naked to the waist, wore a black cavalryman's hat on his head. Another wore a soldier's blue coat. There were four in all, and one was pointing toward the three on the valley floor.

Clyde held himself still with an effort, studying the crest of the ridge behind the Utes, watching for others to join the four. Minutes passed, but he saw nothing.

Relief ran slowly through him. Four to fight, then.

He switched his eyes to Johnny. The boy looked across at him and lifted a hand. Clyde pointed silently behind Johnny, then beckoned slowly and deliberately, hoping that the slowness of his beckoning wave would let Johnny know that Clyde wanted him to move slowly.

Apparently it did. Johnny turned his horse and began to pick his way toward the bottom, as deliberately as though he had all day.

Clyde sat the hillside, frozen, trying to anticipate the course Johnny would take, and the course the Utes would take as they rode toward the bottom.

Their cries, as they surged into motion, rose

like coyote barks in the chill evening air. They thundered downslope toward the three in the bottom, taking a course that would cut the path Johnny was taking near the foot of the ridge.

Lacy and Hawken had dismounted, and were helping Rufe from his horse. They ran fifty yards to a down willow trunk and fell to the ground behind it. Hawken got up, sprinted to his horse and led the animal back to the willow, where he tied it.

Clyde dug spurs into his horse's sides and thundered recklessly toward the bottom. Half a dozen times he looked up, trying to catch Johnny's attention so that he could signal the boy to change course. But Johnny seemed to have eyes only for the three in the bottom.

Nearer and nearer he came to the place where his own and the Indians' trail would meet. And Clyde felt the rise of panic within him. If Johnny didn't stop, if he didn't change course, he'd be dead in a matter of minutes.

Clyde raised his Colt's and fired into the air, fired three times, as fast as he could thumb back the hammer and pull the trigger. And Johnny looked up at last.

Clyde gestured with a frantic waving of his arms, pointed up the hill to Johnny's left, then made a sign for Johnny to stop. There was no use for Johnny to change course. He couldn't possibly reach the three in the bottom before the Indians did. But it might help later to have Johnny at the Indians' rear.

Johnny pulled his horse to a halt, and held him still. Clyde wished he could make out the expression on Johnny's face, wished he could see what was in Johnny's eyes.

The Utes were now almost to the foot of the ridge. In the valley, Lacy and Hawken began to fire at them. Rufe didn't move.

Clyde cursed softly under his breath. They had begun firing too soon. The Utes were still more than four hundred yards from the three, and bullets fired at them now were wasted.

Clyde was riding straight down the hill now, spurring his horse unmercifully. The horse plunged and slid on his haunches, thoroughly terrified and fighting desperately to maintain his footing. Clyde had eyes only for the terrain before him, and he guided the horse with expert care.

Near the foot of the ridge, where it leveled slightly, he raised his eyes. The Utes had reached the valley floor and were streaking across it toward the dead willow trunk behind which Lacy and Rufe and Hawken lay.

Clyde lifted his glance still further and saw Johnny's horse standing riderless in a little grove of scrub oak. Searching, he found Johnny, kneeling behind a rock. As he watched, Johnny's gun puffed smoke, and down in the valley one of the Ute's horses somersaulted violently, throwing his rider clear.

In spite of his anxiety, a smile touched Clyde's thin mouth. Then he broke out of the brush and timber into the valley proper. Down toward the river he plunged, and raced his horse across a wide shallows. The horse's hoofs raised a huge spray of water that drenched Clyde thoroughly. Then he was scrambling out on the other side.

Still in the willows, Clyde yanked him to a rearing halt. He flung himself from the horse, yanking the Spencer from the boot. He tied the horse to a tree, ran to the edge of the willows and flung himself prone.

Out there behind the trunk of that down tree, Lacy would be terrified, he knew. More than anything in the world, he wanted to be out there with her. But he could not possibly have reached her before the Utes cut him off. And he could help her more from here than he could in the open, trying to ride through the party of Indians to reach her.

The Utes thundered on past the place where Lacy and the others were and circled, yelling crazily. Clyde saw now that they were all dressed in remnants of Cavalry uniforms. One wore a blue forage cap. All three of them had yellow kerchiefs tied around their bronzed throats. If they had wounds, they were minor ones, for

Clyde could see neither bandages nor disabilities among them.

They were almost ludicrous, so dressed, their faces and chests painted, their long braids flying out from beneath their captured hats. But there was also, about them, a savage splendor not duplicated in anything Clyde had ever seen before.

He drew a bead on the one with the cavalry officer's black hat and squeezed the trigger. The Ute dropped his Winchester and clutched his chest. He swayed in the saddle, then toppled forward clinging to the horse's mane. The three thundered on upriver out of range and halted to talk. Apparently they had thought they had only the three in the valley to contend with. Now they knew of Johnny, behind them, and Clyde, concealed in the river bottom.

The horse Johnny had downed lay kicking in the deep grass a hundred yards from Clyde's three companions. The brave who had ridden it was crawling along through the grass toward the whites behind the log. Clyde took a shot at him but the range was too great. He missed cleanly.

He saw Johnny run to his horse, mount and ride again toward the bottom, spurring recklessly, jumping his horse over obstructions, sliding sometimes, nearly falling once or twice.

Clyde lunged to his feet and sprinted toward his own horse. He untied the reins swiftly and swung to the saddle. He plunged the horse out of the willows and into the open.

Immediately the two unwounded braves upriver swung their horses and kicked them into motion, heading along a course that would intercept Clyde. Behind the log, Lacy and Hawken began to fire again, but they made no hits. The braves came on.

A strange sense of unreality possessed Clyde as he rode. The scene before him was gray in the fading light. The crawling brave in the grass, Johnny thundering toward him, the two Indians riding hard to intercept Clyde, all seemed unreal.

Smoke puffed from one of the Utes' Winchesters, and something hummed close to Clyde's head. But he didn't slow and he didn't turn. He had to reach that Indian in the grass before Johnny did. Johnny didn't realize it, but a man on horseback makes a fine target for a man on the ground, particularly when the rider is coming directly toward the one on the ground.

Johnny, on the other hand, riding a galloping horse, had little or no chance of hitting the brave on the ground.

Clyde swung his head toward Lacy and the others, behind the willow log. Lacy was firing at the two who were trying to cut Clyde off. Rufe was apparently unconscious, or dead. Hawken was just watching now, making no attempt to even the odds. Up-river, the brave Clyde had wounded, sat his horse with his head down, with his shoulders slumped. This one, Clyde knew, was badly, perhaps mortally wounded. He constituted no threat.

Johnny was now less than a hundred yards from the Indian on the ground. Clyde raised in his stirrups and bellowed, "Johnny No! Let me take him!"

But Johnny didn't hear. He raised his rifle and fired at the man on the ground. The bullet kicked up dust a full ten feet from the prostrate man.

The Indian rolled to face Johnny, bringing up his Winchester. Clyde yelled frantically, "Johnny! Turn!"

But Johnny didn't turn. His face, which Clyde could see clearly now, was intent and set. He raised his rifle again, this time sighting carefully along its barrel.

He never fired. The Winchester in the Indian's hands puffed smoke, and instantly Johnny fell limply sideways. He tumbled from the saddle and hit the ground on one shoulder. For several long seconds his foot hung in the stirrup and the horse dragged him, bumping and sliding along the ground. Then his foot came loose. He rolled, skidded, and came to a halt, as still as death.

Fury soared in Clyde's brain. Before it all thought, all caution, everything fled. Holding rifle and reins in his left hand, he drew his revolver with his right. A dozen yards from the single Ute, he flung himself from his saddle.

So suddenly was the maneuver completed that the horse had no time to stop. Clyde's feet went out from under him and he fell, sliding. But he released neither the rifle nor his revolver. Rising, he flung a snap shot at the brave, whose rifle was coming into line.

The rifle discharged an instant after Clyde's revolver. The bullet passed close enough to be heard as an angry buzz, gone almost before Clyde could realize he had heard it. He brought the revolver up and fired again, this time aiming carefully.

The Ute's throat gushed blood and he clutched it with his hands. Valle didn't even wait for him to fall, but swung around to face the other two.

The revolver clicked on an empty, and Valle dropped it. He swung the Spencer to his shoulder, sighted on the leading Ute and fired. His bullet broke the brave's right arm just above the elbow. It began to swing crazily like a limp, empty sleeve.

Then they were past him, one on one side, one on the other. They galloped off a couple of hundred yards and halted.

Of the four, only one remained unhurt. His companion's right arm was broken. The Ute who had shot Johnny was dead. Looking east, Clyde saw a riderless Indian pony. Then that one, the one he had shot from the willows, was down too, probably also dead.

The two Indians hesitated only an instant. Then they whirled their horses and galloped down-river.

Over behind the willow log, Hawken moved at last. He jumped to his feet, untied his horse and swung to the saddle. He jumped the horse over the log and thundered downriver in pursuit of the disappearing braves.

Clyde went to Johnny and knelt beside him. He pulled back Johnny's shirt. There was a hole in Johnny's chest on the right side. A light froth bubbled from the hole.

Clyde could hear Lacy sobbing brokenly as she ran toward him. He could feel a smarting in his own eyes. He said, "Johnny you did real good. You couldn't have done better if you'd been at this for years."

Johnny opened his eyes. They were tortured and flat with pain. His lips made a twisted smile. "I was scared. I was awful scared."

"I wouldn't have known it from watchin' you."

Distantly, down-river, he heard a shot and said, "That'll be Hawken. He went after the two that were left so they couldn't bring back help."

He heard another shot. He listened a moment, but all was still. Lacy reached him and flung herself down beside him. "Johnny! Oh God!"

Clyde slipped an arm around her shoulder.

Johnny's eyes clung to his face with complete faith. "I'll be all right, won't I Clyde?"

Clyde swallowed. His smile was like a grimace. He swallowed again and said hoarsely, "You'll be all right, kid."

Lacy buried her face in her hands. Clyde reached out and found Johnny's hand with his own. "Hold on, kid. Just hold on."

Johnny gripped his hand weakly for a moment, and then his grip relaxed. Johnny Sauls was dead.

CHAPTER 14

FOR a long time Clyde and Lacy Quaintance knelt beside Johnny's body. Lacy wept, but there was restraint in her weeping, as though she wished to make no sound that would intrude upon the stillness in the air.

Clyde looked at Johnny's boyish face, so still now in death. He was seeing Johnny, not as he was today, but as he had been when he was small. Sadness welled up in him, and a bitter sense of loss. Gradually it was replaced by a feeling of self-blame. Nothing on earth was worth Johnny's life—not money, nor Carrie, nor position nor security.

He felt as guilty as though he had killed Johnny himself. And for the first time, a doubt was born in his mind, doubt of Carrie, who had asked that they do this, who must have known they could not refuse.

He looked at Lacy. Tears had streaked the dust on her face. Her hair was a tousled mop; her eyes were swimming in tears. He was waiting for her to say, "Was it worth it, Clyde? Was it worth Johnny's life?" He waited, and held his glance steady, knowing he would flinch in spite of himself when she said the words.

She didn't say them. Instead she murmured with genuine compassion, "Clyde, I'm sorry. I'm awfully sorry. But you couldn't know it would be like this. Even Carrie couldn't have known. Johnny insisted on coming along. Don't blame yourself."

"Who else shall I blame?" he asked bitterly.

Her face twisted, and she looked away. "What are we going to do, Clyde? What are we going to do?"

His voice was harsh. "The only thing we can. Go on. Neither Hawken nor those other two would let us pull out now."

She didn't reply. Her eyes clung to his face with utter dependence and faith.

Hawken came galloping up the valley grinning, waving a pair of fresh scalps. He glanced at Johnny briefly, asking, "Dead?"

Clyde nodded.

"Too bad," Hawken said perfunctorily. He displayed the scalps. "These two won't bring no help."

Clyde said angrily, "Get those damned things out of sight!" He added, then, "Did you hide the bodies?"

"Dragged 'em down in the willows along the river. Stripped their horses an' turned 'em loose."

Clyde nodded. He got to his feet, seeming to

forget Hawken, and asked of Lacy, “How’s Rufe?”

“He passed out when he hit ground behind that log.”

“Go see how he is.”

Lacy left quickly, without looking at Johnny again. Clyde told Hawken, “Get that one that was wearing the black hat and hide his body, as you hid the others. I’ll take care of this one.”

Hawken rode away. Clyde lifted the body of the Ute and slung him over his saddle. Leading the horse and steadying the body with one hand, he walked to the river. Here he slid the body off and concealed it in the brush. They’d have to take a chance on buzzards, he guessed.

Then he had an inspiration. He mounted and rode to a cow that stood alone not far away. He eased his rifle from the boot and shot the cow in the neck. Now, if the Utes saw buzzards circling this spot, they’d also see the cow and would probably assume that other cows besides this one had been killed down beside the river.

He rode back to Lacy and Rufe. Lacy was bathing Rufe’s face with water from a canteen. Rufe was conscious, but he seemed to have no knowledge of what had taken place, and Clyde didn’t enlighten him.

Hawken returned and caught the horse belonging to the Ute that had killed Johnny. He had to rope it. He stripped it and turned it loose. It trotted westward down the valley.

Clyde told Lacy, "Stay here with Rufe. I'm going to take care of Johnny."

He rode to the boy's body and wrapped it in one of Johnny's own blankets. He lifted it to his saddle and tied it down. Mounting behind it, he rode down-river, skirting the scattering herd. So far he had seen nothing of Blake and Arnold. The fact that he hadn't suddenly made him furiously angry. They hadn't even tried to help in the skirmish with the Indians. Maybe Johnny would still be alive if they had.

The clouds were breaking a little in the west, and the setting sun shone faintly through, appearing like a luminous ball. Perhaps it wouldn't snow after all. Shivering, he went on. Tonight he'd see if Lacy couldn't mend his torn jacket.

A quarter of a mile beyond the cattle, he dismounted. Working swiftly against the coming dark, he began to dig Johnny's grave, using his knife to break the earth, his hands to scoop it out.

Dusk deepened into dark, but still he worked. When it was two feet deep, he stopped. He rested a moment, then unloaded Johnny's body.

Mounting, he rode back to Lacy and Hawken and Rufe. He said, "Lacy, come with me. Hawken, you stay with Rufe."

Hawken didn't protest or argue. Lacy mounted and followed Clyde westward down the valley.

A feeling of depression came over Clyde as he rode. He wished he could live the past week over again, but he couldn't. Instead, he had to live with guilt over Johnny's death. It would always be with him.

At the grave site, he dismounted, turned and helped Lacy to alight. He said, "I want to bury him here so we can drive the cattle over the grave in the morning. That way, it won't be found."

She didn't reply. Clyde asked, "Do you know the words to say, Lacy?"

"No, Clyde. I'm sorry. I just can't seem to think."

"I'll try, then," he said.

He cleared his throat. He hesitated, then said slowly and soberly, "The Lord is my shepherd, I shall not want. He maketh me to lie down in . . ." His voice went on, the only sound in this vast, hushed, empty land.

When he had finished, he lifted Johnny's body in his arms and laid it gently, if awkwardly, in the grave. He was surprised at how little Johnny weighed. "Go on back to the others, Lacy," he said.

She hesitated. "Couldn't I wait?"

"All right." He watched her walk away, leading the two horses. He got on his kness and began to push dirt into the grave with his hands. When he had covered the body, he pushed the rest in with his feet, mounding it over and tramping it down.

He went to Lacy and took the reins of his own horse from her. "We'll not bother to gather on the hillsides tomorrow. We'll take what we have and whatever else we find in the valley, and push on through."

"Do you think we'll find anyone at the Indian agency?"

"No."

"How far?"

"We're probably not more than two or three miles from the agency now. Tomorrow, by moving fast, we ought to get well past it—almost to the edge of the reservation on the other side."

He helped her mount and rode beside her past the herd which was settling down for the night. Reaching the place they had left Rufe and Hawken, Clyde helped Rufe to his saddle and the four rode across the valley to the northern side where he found a grove of scrub-oak in which they could camp.

The venison was gone, but Clyde had a slab of bacon in his saddlebags and some flour. Neither was palatable uncooked, so they settled immediately into their blankets. Clyde left the others, picketed out the horses, then rode his own mount out into the valley. Sitting with his back to a tree, he dozed the night out, alone.

Back in camp, Hawken did not sleep immediately. Until the skirmish with the Utes, he had planned to break away from Clyde and the others and team up with Blake and Arnold. A third share of the herd was what he'd get from them. Clyde had promised him only a sixth.

However, with Johnny's death, the picture had changed considerably. Now there remained only Rufe, who was wounded and sick enough to present no threat to Hawken, and Lacy and Clyde.

If he stayed with them and helped them gather their herd and drive it from the reservation, he might well wind up with the whole works, with Lacy thrown in to boot. Only Clyde could stand in the way. On the other hand, another skirmish with Indians might mean the end of all three. In that case, he knew he'd have to team up with the two horseracers. But, he thought, he'd cross that bridge if and when he came to it.

Hawken was pleased with himself tonight. The way things looked, he was going to run a bit of careless saloon talk into a fortune. And a fortune, at that, which no one would be hunting him for stealing.

In addition, he'd get the satisfaction of killing Clyde, whom he had grown to hate with virulent intensity. He'd get Lacy, who was a cute little thing in spite of her extreme youth. He'd keep her as long as she pleased him.

Under his blankets, he flexed his hands. The bandages were dirty and stiff. But the hands pained him less now. They were still sore, but not sufficiently so to hinder him in anything he wanted to do. His head had ached for hours after the fight with Clyde, but it had stopped now, thank God.

Clyde might be tough, but he was a fool. He was fool enough to trust people, and Hawken had discovered long ago the error of that point of view. Clyde would discover it soon.

He grinned to himself in the darkness. Thirty thousand dollars! It was enough to make a man catch his breath. And it was almost in his grasp!

He slept, and woke, and got up, grinning at his thoughts of the fortune which would soon belong to him.

Rufe seemed stronger this morning, but Lacy had obviously slept little during the night. Clyde, too, was plainly tired, for his face was haggard and drawn, his eyes sunken.

That, Hawken thought, was another thing in his favor. Clyde would now become progressively more exhausted with each passing night. Rufe couldn't stand guard. Clyde wouldn't risk Lacy's safety enough to let her do it. Nor would he trust Hawken to do it. Which left only himself. By the time another two nights had passed, Clyde would be dead on his feet. He'd be an easy mark.

How to get rid of Blake and Arnold troubled

Hawken for a time. But then he put them from his mind. One problem at a time. Secure the herd and get rid of Clyde and Rufe first. Then decide what to do about the unscrupulous pair of horse-racers.

He left camp to get the horses. Not quite out of earshot, he heard Clyde and Lacy begin to talk in subdued tones. . . .

Clyde looked at Lacy's drawn, worried face. He wanted to take her in his arms. He wanted to reassure her.

She asked quietly, "What do you think Hawken will do now, Clyde?"

He shrugged. "I doubt if he'll do anything until we get out of the reservation. He's greedy, Lacy, and that's in our favor. If he wasn't greedy, he'd change sides. He'd go over to Arnold and Blake right now. But he wants the whole herd for himself. So he'll wait." He frowned. "The trouble is, he's going to be rested and fresh when we leave the reservation, and the rest of us are going to be so damned tired we can hardly stand up."

"I'll help you stand guard tonight."

He shook his head. "You've got enough, taking care of Rufe. How many times were you up with him last night?"

She smiled. "Several. But I don't mind."

"He looks better this morning. Is he?"

Lacy shook her head. "His mind is wandering.

He thinks he's back in Georgia, fighting the war. He ought to have some food."

"I'll kill a calf tonight. Maybe we'll be far enough downriver by then so that we can have a fire."

He stared wearily at the murmuring river below him. He knew how little chance they had with Hawken in their midst, with Blake and Arnold waiting until the time was right, with Indians all around. The job would have been tough enough if he'd had a trustworthy crew of hardened men to do it. With no more than he had, with treachery a certainty, the chances he'd get out with the cattle were almost non-existent.

He clenched his jaw, hard. Maybe he wouldn't get out with the cattle. But he'd get out with Lacy and Rufe, or die trying.

Hawken returned, leading the horses. Clyde led Rufe's to him and boosted Rufe to the saddle. Rufe's shoulder was freshly bandaged. He looked at Clyde without recognition. Clyde said, "Stick it out today, Rufe, the best you can. By tonight, maybe we'll be far enough away so that we can hole up and rest a few days."

"We retreatin', sonny?"

Clyde said, "No, Rufe. There's more fighting ahead."

"You're a replacement, ain't you? Ain't they even givin' the recruits uniforms these days?"

Clyde shook his head and turned away. Lacy

had mounted, and so had Hawken. Clyde swung to his own saddle and rode down into the valley to begin bunching the cattle. As he did, he scanned the hillsides carefully.

He felt responsibility for Rufe's condition heavily. And this morning, if he'd thought he could get away with it, he'd have taken Rufe and Lacy, left the herd and ridden out of the reservation. But he knew Hawken and Blake and Arnold would never let them go.

Slowly he and Hawken bunched the cattle, slowly got them moving. The herd strung out, and Clyde took a rough tally of them in his mind as they did. He guessed their number well over five hundred. Probably they'd pick up another two or three hundred by the time they reached the Agency. And that would have to do. He couldn't risk trying to gather the slopes. He wouldn't leave Lacy alone in the valley, with only Rufe for protection.

Remembering Johnny's grave, Clyde turned the herd slowly and drove them across it. After they had passed, it was impossible to tell where the grave had been.

He noticed Lacy looking back afterward. It hurt her, he knew, to think that even Johnny's grave was lost, for now it must seem to her that Johnny had never existed at all.

Yet there had been a good reason for hiding Johnny's grave. Indians were not above disinterring a body to mutilate and scalp it. And Clyde couldn't bear to think of them doing that to Johnny.

He saw the haze of smoke again as the sun came up in the east. Topping a slight rise, he saw the still-smoldering buildings of the White River Agency ahead. Beside the remains of the building were cultivated fields, fenced against cattle, but ruined now by the Indians.

Corn and ripe oats fields were trampled, as though a herd of cattle had been driven through. On the south side of the valley, Clyde could see part of an Indian racetrack. The other part had been plowed up.

He began to turn the herd northward so that they could drive past the agency without actually going among the buildings or through the fields. He saw a couple of gray wolves slink away from one of the buildings and disappear on the sagebrush-covered hillside.

Lacy left Rufe's side and rode to him. Her face was white. "Clyde, I'm going down there. Someone might need our help."

He shook his head. "Stay with Rufe. I'll go."

He turned his horse aside, reined in, and watched the cattle stream on toward the hillside. The valley was narrower here. Across it and across the river, he could see a well-worn trail ascending toward the pass that led southward to Grand River. Somewhere up there the whole Ute tribe was camped. This was, perhaps, the most perilous part of the whole journey, for any Utes traveling between their camp and the battle must pass through here.

He studied the rising country to the south for a long time before he rode on down among the blackened ruins of the Indian Agency. He saw nothing.

The Utes had been thorough in their destruction of the agency. Not a building remained unburned. Farming machinery lay scattered about, part of it wrecked, part of it burned. Here was a rake with the wheels bent almost flat with the ground. Here was a plow, its oakbeam burned and only its plow-share and hardware remaining. Half a dozen buzzards rose, flapping noisily, from behind one of the blackened log buildings. Rounding the corner, Clyde saw another wolf slink away.

The smell of death was strong in his nostrils. His horse fidgeted and danced uneasily, frightened by buzzard and wolf smell, made uneasy by the strong, sweet smell of death.

The carrion eaters had partially destroyed the evidences of Indian mutilation and barbarity, but they had not destroyed them altogether. There was still enough here for Clyde to see, still enough to suddenly remove any lingering guilt he might have felt over killing the Indian two nights back, over the killing of the four Indians yesterday evening.

In spite of himself, his stomach churned as he looked down from his horse at the half-dozen bodies lying on the ground. Stripped and scalped, they seemed hardly human. Stakes had been driven into two of them. Others had been mutilated with knives.

He circled through the smoldering ruins for about ten minutes, calling out, listening and hearing nothing. Finally, deciding that nothing here remained alive, he headed up the low hill-side to northward in the wake of the slow-moving herd.

CHAPTER 15

THE SUN was now high in the sky. Of yesterday's storm, which had not materialized, there now remained only a few high, wispy clouds. The smell of the dead at the agency seemed to stay in Clyde's nostrils, cloying and heavily depressing.

He halted on a promontory and searched the valley to the east. Another hour, he thought. Another hour and we'll be out of sight of this place. Another hour and we'll be reasonably safe, from the Utes at least.

His eyes swung, and he studied the rising land to the south.

Up there, he could see the plain-marked trail as clearly as though it were a road. It wound back and forth, dipping occasionally into ravines, coming out again. There seemed to be a haze of dust about a mile away where the trail dipped into a deep ravine.

Suddenly he stiffened. For he saw, coming out of the ravine, the antlike figures of a dozen or more horsemen.

His immediate inclination was to whirl and set

his spurs. But he realized at once that any sudden movement here would surely draw the attention of those distant horsemen.

Turning his head, he picked himself a route through the low, rounded hills which would keep him partly concealed from the Utes. Then he swung to the ground.

Eastward, he caught a glimpse of either Blake or Arnold, moving through the trees. They were on the south slope, then, and had not yet seen the Utes. But he wasn't going to worry about them. Let them shift for themselves.

Leading his horse, he picked his way along the route he had chosen. Entering a grove of cedars, he swung again to the saddle and spurred wildly.

A few moments later he caught up with Lacy and Hawken and Rufe. He called, "Utes! Get off your horses and lead them over here. They haven't seen us yet, and maybe they won't if we stay quiet."

All heads swung to the south. Lacy and Hawken dismounted immediately. Clyde helped Rufe to the ground.

He led them behind the rounded knob of a low hill and they tied their horses in the high sagebrush. Hawken had an odd grin on his face. "Have you seen them two—Blake and Arnold?"

Clyde nodded. "I saw one of them over on the south slope about half a mile from the gap."

The cattle moved on slowly, spreading out to

graze. Clyde hoped that by the time the war party of Utes arrived, the cattle would be dispersed enough so that it would not be apparent they were being driven. Yet he also realized that the Utes could scarcely fail to wonder at such a concentration of cattle here in this one spot.

Rufe collapsed on the ground to rest. He was sweating and his face was pale. He looked at Clyde without recognition.

Hawken wormed his way up the side of the knoll until he could see over the top. He turned and beckoned to Clyde. Then he slid his rifle out ahead of him,

Lacy sat down beside Rufe and began to open his shirt so that she could look at the bandage. Clyde studied Hawken's back, wondering at the odd smile he'd seen on Hawken's face.

He eased up the knoll, crawling the last few yards, and came up beside Hawken. The file of warriors, decked out for battle, was now entering the valley.

There were about twenty of them, headed, Clyde supposed, for the battle up north. They splashed across the river. Apparently they had paid no attention to the cattle, a large number of which were now hidden by the tall sagebrush in which they were grazing.

Thank God he and the others had gotten past the agency before that party of braves showed up.

He noticed that Hawken's grip on his rifle was

unusually tight. The grin remained on Hawken's face.

Clyde wondered what was in the big man's mind. Did he intend to betray their location to the Utes with a shot, counting on speed to get away? Was this what he had in mind by way of getting rid of Lacy and Rufe and Clyde himself?

Clyde didn't know. But suddenly he was tired of wondering about Hawken, tired of waiting for the man to act.

He eased his revolver from its holster. He jammed its muzzle hard against Hawken's side and thumbed back the hammer. "Your rifle—throw it back down the hill behind you."

"I wasn't . . ."

"Maybe not. But I'm taking no chance. It'd be real easy for you to let them know we were here. You figure we'd hold them up long enough for you to get away, don't you?"

"That wasn't what I was thinkin' at all." Hawken rolled partway and tossed his rifle from him.

"That's better," Clyde watched the Indians narrowly. They turned while still short of the burned agency buildings and headed east.

He didn't see how they could avoid noticing the trail of shod hoofs overlying the tracks of the cattle when they crossed them. Beside him, Hawken asked, the incident of the rifle apparently forgotten, "Where did you see Blake and Arnold?"

Clyde looked across at the far slope. "See that lightning-struck pine? They were about a hundred yards east of that when I saw them. They can't be far from the pine right now if they saw the Indians. And I don't see how they could have missed seeing them."

He put his glance on the Indians again. Hawken continued to study the slope. At last he murmured, "I see them. They're off to the right of the pine about fifty yards. See?"

Clyde looked. He saw a horse, and what looked like two men lying behind the trunk of a down tree. Except for the height of the knoll he and Hawken were on, he would have seen neither.

But his thoughts wouldn't stay on either Blake or Arnold. He stared down at the Indians and began to sweat.

Tension built in him. Indians skirted the ravaged grainfields and rode toward the half-plowed racetrack east of the agency buildings. Several of them raced their horses around the unplowed portion of it, waving Winchesters over their heads, whooping and yelling noisily. Clyde turned his head and grinned reassuringly at Lacy, who looked completely terrified.

Now the Indians were leaving the racetrack and crossing the valley. Now they were crossing the trail of the driven cattle.

They were well east of the agency now, almost a mile east. But there, in the middle of the trail which the cattle had left, they halted abruptly. One of them pointed at the ground.

They milled around for a few moments. Their shouts came faintly to Clyde's ears. Then, as though decided, they lined out on the trail of the cattle, galloping directly toward Clyde and Hawken.

Clyde released a long breath. He said, "We're in for it now. Come on. Let's get ready."

He slid back off the knoll out of sight and got to his feet. Hawken had preceded him. Hawken snatched up his rifle and ran for his horse.

Clyde hurried to Lacy. "Get your rifle. Give one to Rufe. It looks like this is it."

She hurried to the horses, snatched her rifle from the boot and afterwards got Rufe's. Clyde helped Rufe to his feet and half carried him back toward the knoll. He knew they had no chance. He also knew they'd die fighting. No one surrendered to Indians.

He forgot Hawken for the moment. He got Rufe in place at the crest of the knoll. As he did, Lacy came crawling toward him, a rifle in each hand.

Suddenly he heard the rapid beat of hoofs. Glancing around, he saw Hawken galloping around the side of the knoll.

His eyes widened with surprise. He had expected, if anything, that Hawken would flee. Instead the man was galloping straight down into the valley, directly at the approaching Utes.

Their whoops of triumph were clearly audible as they sighted him. They changed course immediately to try and intercept him.

Clyde breathed, "What's the matter with him? Has he gone nuts?"

Lacy didn't reply. She was watching Hawken, fascinated.

With a score of howling Utes close on his heels, Hawken crossed the valley, plunged through the river and disappeared into the timber on the far side. A volley of shots racketed from the Indian's guns.

Clyde could follow Hawken's progress through the timber by catching a glimpse of him now and again as he crossed some small clearing. Almost at once, his destination became plain. He was heading straight toward the two horseracers, Blake and Arnold.

What was in the man's mind, Clyde couldn't imagine. He watched, breathless, as Hawken continued up the hill.

And then, at last, he understood. Because Hawken didn't pause as he reached the pair. He went on, instead, and moments later disappeared over the top of the ridge.

The Utes, close behind him, slammed into a fusillade of bullets from Blake's and Arnold's guns.

Three went down in the first volley of shots.

The others bunched, milled for the briefest instant, then whirled and galloped away.

They dismounted as soon as they were hidden by timber and brush. Afoot, they began to creep toward the hidden pair of whites.

Lacy breathed, “Hawken led the Indians right to them!”

Clyde nodded. “It’s only a matter of time. The Utes will circle around behind them. They haven’t got a chance.”

“Hawken saved our lives.”

“He traded them—traded them for Blake and Arnold’s lives. Don’t fool yourself, Lacy. We’re not safe yet. The only reason Hawken did it was that he wanted Blake and Arnold out of the way. He thinks he can kill Rufe and me and take you and the cattle for himself.”

Lacy shuddered. She watched the scene on the far hillside with widened eyes.

The Indians now had the pair encircled, and were moving in. Occasionally either Blake or Arnold would fire at a half-hidden shape, but they made no hits.

Movement in the valley that led southward to the Indian’s camp caught Clyde’s eye. He saw Hawken ride across it and lose himself in the timber on the far side. Hawken was safe, now. Then he’d return. When he did, Clyde knew he’d better be ready for the man.

The utter cold-bloodedness of Hawken’s

maneuver appalled him. Hawken had killed Blake and Arnold as surely as though he had pulled the trigger himself.

Nor was it, necessarily, over. The Utes, after disposing of Blake and Arnold, might still decide to investigate the trail they had been following when Hawken diverted them.

Suddenly he saw one of the white men on the far hillside rise to his feet. Distance was too great to see which of them it was.

He staggered a few feet, then collapsed on the ground. A chorus of yells rose on the still air, sounding almost like coyote barks. Clyde scowled.

The other man rose from behind the down log and sprinted for his horse. He never made it. Guns roared, and he fell as though driven by a mighty blow from behind.

The Indians came out into the open now, rushing in to take scalps and count coup. For a few moments they were busy beside the bodies of the two white men. Clyde glanced at Lacy. Her face was white and set. She knew, as well as he, what the Utes were doing now. They were mutilating the bodies.

Clyde breathed, "Now we'll see. We'll see how successful Hawken's trick was."

They watched the Indians bunch and load their dead. A couple of them headed up the ridge, leading the horses packed with the bodies of the dead. These would return to the villages, Clyde knew.

The others mounted and milled around for several moments. Then they galloped recklessly down the ridge toward the valley.

In the middle of it, they halted. One pointed along the trail they had been following when Hawken diverted them.

Even at this distance, their arguing voices were audible to Clyde. He held his breath, waiting. If the Indians should decide to investigate the trail, he and Lacy and Rufe were finished.

But, on the other hand, there was a chance that the Indians would not investigate the trail. They might assume that Hawken and the other two they had just killed had made the tracks. Furthermore, they were flushed with victory and with excitement. Perhaps they would be anxious enough to join the battle with the troops to ignore the chance of further victories here.

The argument in the valley was over almost as quickly as it had begun. One of the Indians rode out at a dead run and the others followed. They disappeared into the timber on the north side of the valley.

Lacy released a long, shuddering sigh of relief. Clyde said, “Stay where you are. They’re tricky. Could be they did that just to throw us off guard. They might be easing back this way through the timber.”

"Clyde, let's go, please. Let's get out of here."

He shook his head. "Hawken's downriver. The Indians are upriver. We've got to stay put."

"You think Hawken might do the same thing to us that he did to Blake and Arnold?"

"I doubt it. It wouldn't work twice. Next time they might leave half their party to take care of us while the other half took after Hawken. He won't chance it. He thinks he can take care of us all by himself."

They lay still, hardly breathing, for another fifteen minutes. Clyde's ears were tuned to the sounds around him. But he heard nothing.

At last he got up. He said softly, "I think the Indians are gone, but I'm going to scout around and see. Sit tight."

He caught his horse and mounted. He quartered up the hillside in the direction the Indians had gone.

He rode for about a mile in a northeasterly direction. At last he topped the ridge. Careful not to show himself, he eased along to a place from which he could see the spread of land to the north. He saw the party of Indians, now several miles away, and breathed a long sigh of relief. Then he turned to go back to Lacy and to the problem of the treacherous Hawken.

Hawken returned toward the place he had left the others cautiously. He did not delude himself that he had fooled Clyde. But he felt triumphant.

He had disposed of Blake and Arnold neatly. The idea of how to do it, coming over him suddenly back there, had been a stroke of genius.

Now, all that lay between him and the entire herd was Clyde. Rufe didn't even know where he was or what was happening. Lacy, once Clyde was dead, would accept the inevitable.

Actually, Hawken would need Lacy. One man just couldn't manage a herd as large as this. But one man and a woman could.

Rufe was a stumbling block, not one, however, that couldn't be removed. Hell, he wasn't going to baby Rufe along, or even let Lacy do it. He needed her to help drive the cattle. So Rufe would have to go.

Short of the place he had left the others by a quarter mile, Hawken dismounted. From there he proceeded on foot, slipping from tree to tree, walking as silently as his size and bulk would permit.

Tension rose in him. He was firmly convinced that Clyde Valle was a fool, without the ruthlessness to do what needed to be done. But he couldn't be sure his opinion of Clyde was right. The man had surprised him before. He might again. With his back to a wall, Clyde might exhibit a ruthlessness Hawken did not anticipate.

He was also aware that by advancing on Clyde, he was putting himself at a disadvantage. Clyde might be waiting for him in any of a hundred ambushes, waiting silently and completely hidden.

Nervously, he cast his glance from left to right. He saw nothing.

He held his rifle before him, finger on the trigger, ready to swing and fire it with instant precision.

He could only hope that the war party of Indians would be out of earshot. But that was a chance he'd have to take.

He heard a twig crack behind him and off to his left, and swung like a cat toward it. His ears caught a hissing sound, one he could not immediately place, and uneasiness crawled in his mind.

Then, a corner of his eye caught movement, and he saw Clyde standing there behind him. His eyes caught something else, too, something coming toward him through the air.

He ducked instinctively, but not quickly enough. The noose of Clyde's rope settled over his head.

His rifle was in position to fire, but he did not fire. His arms went up instinctively, helplessly, to ward off the settling noose.

And then it yanked tight around his throat.

He was jerked off balance and fell. The rough noose burned the skin of his neck. It tightened savagely, until he was being dragged along the ground. His breath shut off; the cry he tried to utter died in his throat, a gagging gurgle.

He clung to his rifle, trying to roll, trying to bring it to bear. He felt a savage kick strike his right forearm, numbing it, and the gun fell out of his hand.

Clyde stood over him, and now, with his hands free, Hawken clawed at the noose around his neck.

It loosened, and air flowed again into his lungs. He looked at Clyde with more pure hatred than he had ever felt before. He said, "You son-of-a-bitch! You can't stay awake forever. And when you do sleep . . ."

Clyde kicked him, hard, in the ribs. Hawken clamped his jaws shut. Clyde said harshly, "Get up. We're going on."

CHAPTER 16

THEY drove until dusk at a fast clip, and by the time they halted, Clyde estimated they had come more than fifteen miles from the burned and gutted Agency. He also guessed that, practically speaking, there was now little danger from Indians.

He therefore caught a calf and killed it with his knife. He skinned and gutted the carcass and carried it into camp.

There should have been jubilation in him tonight. He and the others had done the impossible; they'd driven nearly a thousand cattle out from under the very noses of the Utes.

Blake and Arnold no longer threatened. Except for the threat Hawken presented, there should be nothing but clear sailing ahead.

But Clyde could feel no jubilation, for the price had been too high. Johnny Sauls was dead.

He missed Johnny tremendously. And he felt a continuation of the depressed foreboding that had troubled him for the past several days.

He picketed all the horses but his own, gathered wood and built a fire. Then he stared out across the valley at the herd, now settling down for the night.

The fire crackled pleasantly and cheerfully. Clyde realized suddenly how ravenous he was.

Hawken dozed nearby, sometimes peering inscrutably at Clyde through slitted, half-open eyes. Rufe slept heavily, snoring, his mouth open, his face drawn and pale. Lacy's eyes seemed unusually large as she came to the fire and began to prepare supper. Clyde realized she was thinner than she had been before.

He felt a wave of tenderness toward her, and said quietly, "We'll drive one more day. Then we'll rest."

She nodded without speaking. There was this quality of dumb acceptance about her now. It made Clyde uneasy and vaguely guilty. It was as though Lacy had lost faith, and had only resignation to take their places.

Dark replaced the dusk, and stars came winking out in the velvet sky overhead. A wind stirred along the river.

Clyde cut slices of meat from one of the calf's hind quarters, and Lacy fried them in the skillet. The smell of coffee and frying meat filled the tiny clearing.

Lacy fed Rufe first, and then she and Clyde and Hawken ate together in silence beside the fire. Afterward, Clyde drew Lacy away from the fire and into the shadows beyond, keeping a careful eye on Hawken as he did. "I'm going to get rid of all the guns we've got but three, your rifle and mine, and my six-shooter. I want you to sleep on your rifle and keep it in your hands whenever I'm not around."

"All right, Clyde."

He put his arms around her, hoping the closeness that had been between them two nights before would return. But she stiffened, and pulled away. "Please, Clyde. If I let go, I'll go to pieces."

He released her, troubled. They returned to camp and Clyde gathered up all the weapons except for Lacy's rifle and his own. He mounted and rode down to the river. Splashing out into the middle of it, he dropped the guns into a deep pool. Then he returned to camp. Probably Lacy still wanted him to give up the cattle. But he couldn't now. It would be a betrayal of Johnny, who had given his life to get them. It would be surrendering to Hawken. It would mean that everything they had endured had been for nothing.

Hawken watched him steadily as he entered the clearing. There was an ominous, waiting quality to Hawken's expression.

Clyde studied him truculently. If he left Hawken here in camp and went out to guard the cattle, then Lacy could get no sleep. Also, there was a good chance that Hawken would overpower her and get her rifle. But if he did not guard the cattle, they might stray during the night or in the early morning.

Finally, he settled on the only course possible. He'd tie Hawken up. That way, Lacy would be safe, and he himself could get a little sleep, in snatches at least, while he was out in the valley guarding the herd.

Sleep for him now, he knew, was of paramount importance. If he didn't get it, it was only a matter of time until Hawken would catch him dozing and kill him.

He told Hawken harshly, "Get up and turn your back. I'm going to tie you up."

"The hell you are!"

Clyde said eagerly, "Go ahead. Give me an excuse. It's all I want from you now."

Hawken weighed the expression on Clyde's face. Then he got up. He turned his back sullenly, holding his hands out behind him.

Clyde tied them securely with one of Johnny Saul's bridle reins. He said, "Pick yourself a place to spend the night and I'll tie your feet."

Hawken swung his head and glared. "What about Injuns? What if . . . ?"

"That's a chance you have to take."

Hawken growled something indistinguishable, and went to lie down where his bedroll lay. Watchfully, Clyde tied his ankles. He was not proud of the feelings running through him. He realized that he actually hoped that Hawken would try to kick at him so that he'd be justified in killing the man.

Standing, he understood fully how much anxiety Hawken had caused him during the past several days. Because now, temporarily at least, the anxiety was gone.

He said, "Lacy, the cattle will stay put for now. You get some sleep. I'll stay here until midnight."

She smiled at him gratefully, but protested, "You need it a lot worse than I do. Sleep for a while, Clyde—for a couple of hours at least."

He shook his head.

Lacy frowned at him with exasperation. "Clyde, for heaven's sake, use your head. You know how dangerous it is for you not to sleep. You know he's only waiting until . . ."

He nodded reluctantly. "All right, Lacy. All right."

He laid down, resting his head on a turf hummock. And was instantly asleep.

It seemed only a moment before he felt Lacy shaking him. He sat up quickly, feeling groggy and drugged. "What is it?" he whispered. "What's the matter?"

Lacy's voice was the merest, terrified whisper. "Clyde! There's someone out there in the brush!"

He came to his feet, confused by a dream he'd

been having, startled and alarmed by Lacy's terror. He'd thought they were safe from Indians. Damn it . . .

Hawken was tied and unarmed, and there was no time to release him now. Rufe was snoring noisily.

Lacy whispered, "What are we going to do, Clyde? Oh God, what are we going to do? Suppose they're all around us?"

Clyde put a hand on her shoulder, his senses sharpening. "Where did you hear the noise?" He could see her face in the thin moonlight that sifted through a light layer of clouds overhead. She pointed. "Down there."

Clyde turned his head in that direction and listened intently. He heard a faint rustle of brush, and an odd, half-human sound that made the flesh crawl on the back of his neck.

A chill ran along his spine, and his body broke out in a sudden, cold sweat. Lacy gasped.

He gripped Lacy's arm. "Quiet! Get hold of yourself. Wait it out."

Her body was trembling violently. If Indians were out there—if they were really surrounded—then these might be their last moments together.

He moved his face close to her ear, and whispered almost soundlessly, "Lacy, I love you. I want you to know in case . . ."

The moon edged through a thin spot in the clouds and the light increased slightly. Clyde thought he saw something move half a dozen yards down the slope.

He raised his gun, but he couldn't see the sights. The distance was too great for offhand shooting, so he lowered it again reluctantly.

The blurred shape moved, and the rustling came again. Whatever it was seemed to be crawling on the ground. Nor did Clyde believe it was an animal, for there was no flowing stealth of movement about it. Instead, it seemed to move jerkily and with much effort.

That was odd, he thought. And then, suddenly, because he had been dreaming of Johnny Sauls when Lacy awakened him, the eerie notion came to him that this was Johnny, come from the grave to rejoin his friends.

Clyde's blood seemed cold as ice; his hands felt numb. He scoffed angrily at himself, at the crazy notion. It couldn't be Johnny. Johnny was dead.

The figure came closer, and now Clyde could see that it was a man, crawling with agonizing slowness up the slope toward them.

Clyde raised his gun again. He called softly, "Stop right where you are or I'll blow your brains out."

But the man didn't freeze. He made a kind of sob in his throat and stumbled to his feet. He came toward them at a painful, shambling run, babbling like a maniac, laughing and crying out, "Thank God! You're white! Thank God!"

Clyde relaxed his tense finger from around the trigger and lowered the gun. He swung his head, still wary. "Don't move, Lacy. It could be an Indian trick."

Lacy froze at his side, scarcely daring to breathe.

The man fell, sprawling, the instant before he reached Clyde. Looking down, Clyde dimly saw his matted beard and tangled hair, his torn clothing, his utter and complete exhaustion. He said, "Build up the fire, Lacy. It's all right. He must have gotten away from the Agency when it was attacked."

Lacy busied herself with the fire. A moment later a thin yellow tongue of flame licked up. By this light, Clyde could see the man more clearly.

His week-old crop of whiskers were gray. His face was pointed, his eyes blue and edged with crow's feet wrinkles. When he laughed, he showed not only hysterical relief, but broken and blackened front teeth.

The stranger croaked, "Food. Have you got some food?"

Clyde nodded. "Where'd you come from?"

"White River Indian Agency. I was haulin' dirt for a sod roof when the shootin' began. I saw Meeker shot down on the porch of his house. I ran. I've been crawlin' through this brush for a week. For a while they trailed me, playin' me like a cat plays a mouse. But I got away. You hear? I got away!"

Clyde turned his head. "Cook him some meat, will you, Lacy?"

He was still wary. It seemed impossible that anyone could have survived the massacre at the Agency, or that he could have eluded the Utes afterward.

Suddenly, unexpectedly, the man began to cry like a child. Tears ran across his dirty, lined cheeks. He choked, "Oh my God, I'm glad to see a white face again! I thought I never would. I'm weak, man. I ain't et nothin' but a few grass-hoppers, an' I couldn't keep them down."

Clyde relaxed at last. This man was not bait thrown out by the Utes. He said, "You're all right now. We've got an extra horse. You can stay with us."

He frowned inwardly. Here was a witness against him. But he couldn't turn his back on a man that needed him as this one did.

He turned and helped Lacy prepare the meat. When it was done, he watched Lacy feed it to him.

There was gentleness and pity in her face. But she was firm about making the man chew well and eat slowly. At last she said, "You can have more later. Right now you've had enough. I'll make you some coffee."

The man settled back, putting his shoulder against a tree. He smiled for the first time. "Thank you, ma'am. You're an angel."

Clyde asked, “What’s your name?”

“Clennon. Ed Clennon.”

“You’re the only survivor?”

“I reckon so. Except for the women. The Utes took them, but I reckon they’re all dead too by now.” He glanced at Lacy. “Sorry, ma’am.”

“How’d you find us?”

“Seen you this afternoon from that far hillside. I almost didn’t come down—figured you might be Injuns dressed like white men. Then I thought I better look—an’ I heard you talkin’ English.”

For a few moments Clyde was silent. Then he asked, “You know what we’re doing?”

The man looked at him uncertainly. “Unless you work for the Government, you’re stealin’ cattle.”

Clyde said reluctantly, “I hate to put it this way, but you owe your life to the fact that we’re here. You realize that, don’t you?”

Clennon nodded. Fear began to grow in his eyes.

Clyde said irritably, “For Christ’s sake, don’t look at me like that. I’m not going to kill you. I’m just asking if you’ll keep your mouth shut about this when we reach civilization.”

Clennon nodded. Fear had eased in his eyes, but it hadn’t left him altogether.

Clyde said, “Help us drive, and you’ll get paid for it.”

"All right."

Clyde felt a touch of bleak discouragement. He knew he couldn't trust Clennon's word. He guessed a man with scruples should never undertake a job like this. He asked, "You got a gun?"

Clennon nodded. He pulled a small Colt's revolver from his belt where it had been hidden by his tattered coat. He looked across at Hawken, whose prone body was now illuminated by the growing fire. "Why's he tied?"

Clyde said flatly, "He wants more than a cut of this herd. He wants it all. He'll kill to get it if we give him a chance."

Clennon didn't reply. But judging from his expression, he was wondering how much better off he was here than he had been out in the brush.

CHAPTER 17

HAWKEN lay still on the ground, watching Valle and Clennon beside the fire. The leather bindings around his wrists had cut off circulation, and now both arms tingled maddeningly.

Clyde left the fire, got his horse and rode out into the valley. Lacy wrapped herself in her blankets and laid down on the ground not far from where Rufe was. Clennon sat beside the fire, staring into it. After a while, he got the rest of the meat from the skillet and ate it wolfishly.

He ate too fast. A few moments later he got up and left the fire. Hawken heard him retching out in the darkness.

Lacy stirred, and moaned, but did not waken. After a long time Clennon returned, his face shiny with sweat.

He sat down and stared at the dying fire, its red glow on his face. Hawken said softly, "Come here, Clennon."

"Why?"

"I want to talk to you." Hawken made his voice sound reasonable and calm.

Clennon hesitated, but in the end he got up and came to where Hawken lay. "What do you want?"

Hawken chuckled softly. "You wasn't taken in, was you?"

"What do you mean?"

"I mean by Valle. Hell, man, he can't let either you or me live. He knows damn well one of us or maybe both would go to the sheriff of the first town we came to and tell about the cattle."

"He said he'd give us a share. If we take it, we're as guilty as he is."

Hawken laughed softly. "Is a man guilty that's forced to commit a crime? All we got to do is to say he threatened to kill us if we didn't help."

"He ain't the kind of man that'd . . ."

Hawken interrupted, "Ain't he? That's all you know about him. He killed a fifteen year old boy that was with us last night. And about tomorrow night he'll kill you and me. Unless we get away."

He wished he could see Clennon's face. He said, "You realize how much money is involved in this?"

"Hadn't thought of it." Clennon's voice was hoarse and raspy.

"Figure it out, then. He's got damn near a thousand head of cattle out there in the valley. They're worth at least thirty dollars a head. That's thirty thousand dollars. Men have been murdered for a hell of a lot less than that."

"He said you was the one that was plannin' on killin'."

Hawken laughed contemptuously. "You reckon I can kill anyone without a gun—with my hands and feet tied?"

There was silence for a few moments while Hawken let Clennon's confused badgered mind work. At last he whispered persuasively, "Cut these damn thongs on my hands and feet. We'll catch us a couple of horses and get the hell out of here. You don't have to trust me. You've got a gun and I haven't. We'll ride north and by mornin' we'll both be safe. But if we stay here, it's either be killed by Valle or be guilty of cattle stealin'."

He let Clennon think it over. Then he said urgently, "Don't take too long to make up your mind. There ain't but a couple of hours left 'till dawn."

Clennon moved hesitantly toward him. Hawken felt him fumbling at the thongs on his hands. Clennon didn't have a knife, apparently, so he was untying them.

After what seemed an interminable time, Hawken's hands were free. Clennon bent to untie his feet.

Hawken's muscles tensed. It would take but an instant to overpower Clennon, who was weak from hunger and exposure.

Then he shook his head imperceptibly. No. The

scuffle might rouse Lacy. Hawken's arms would have no strength yet and his feet were still tied.

It would be better to ride off with Clennon. It would be better to wait until Clennon's suspicions were gone.

Clennon finished untying Hawken's feet and helped him rise. Hawken staggered, recovered, and followed Clennon silently toward the place where the horses were picketed. Neither Lacy nor Rufe stirred.

The saddles had been tossed on the ground between camp and the horses. Hawken picked up two at random, and gave one to Clennon. The man was so weak it took him three tries before he got it on the horse's back.

The pair rode out, climbing the ridge north of the river. Feeling began to return to Hawken's arms and legs. They prickled maddeningly for about fifteen minutes.

He rubbed his arms as he rode, and gradually the prickling went away.

Dawn showed itself as a gray line upon the eastern horizon. Clennon, leading, began to bear right a little, following the country, and Hawken called, "Stay left unless you want to run afoul of that battle between the Injuns and the troops."

Clennon changed course.

The sky grew lighter. Clennon called back, "How long you reckon it'll take us to reach Laramie or Steele?"

Hawken said, "Couple of days." But even as he spoke, he was thinking, "You'll never reach it, you dumb bastard."

The sun came up, touching the high peaks with its yellow brilliance. A deer crossed in front of them, less than fifty yards away. By the time Clennon had his gun out, the deer was gone.

Hawken said, "Too bad. You could have used some food. Better let me take that gun in case we see another one."

Clennon glanced around suspiciously, but Hawken wasn't looking at him. Instead, he was carefully studying the land nearby.

They rode on for another mile in silence. Clennon carried the gun in his hand now. Another deer jumped up, and Clennon fired once before the deer disappeared. His bullet missed.

Hawken said nothing.

Clennon reined in. He handed the gun to Hawken. "All right. See if you can hit one. God, I'm hungry!"

Hawken smiled. Clennon moved out, crowding to the left of the trail to let Hawken pass. Hawken raised the gun, aimed at Clennon's back and fired.

Clennon didn't make a sound. He folded forward over the horse's withers as though he were tired or dizzy. Then quietly he slipped from the saddle and hit the ground.

Hawken shoved the gun into his waistband and

dismounted. He knelt beside Clennon and put a hand on his chest. He felt nothing. He got up, and mounted. Then he rode south in the direction they had come, only now, Hawken bore right at an angle that would put him into the valley ahead of Clyde and his herd.

Returning, he could expect Valle to be on guard. He could expect to be searched for Clennon's gun. But if he hid the gun downriver, he could pick it up after Clyde had searched him, and after Clyde's guard was down.

He judged it was about eight o'clock when he reached the river. He halted on a promontory and studied the valley for a while before he rode down. There was a dead cottonwood log at the bottom of the slope that was bare of bark and gleamed whitely in the sun. Faintly smiling, he rode down to it and hid the gun in the grass beside it.

Mounting again, he rode back up the slope to the crest of the ridge. Here, he turned east.

Mile after mile fell behind, and at last, in midmorning, he sighted the cattle in the distance.

He continued until he was abreast of them. He could see Valle and Lacy and Rufe, riding slowly in the wake of the leisurely traveling herd. He turned and rode down the slope.

Clyde looked up as he approached and his hand dropped to his gun. He drew it and thumbed back the hammer. Hawken raised his hands, holding his reins in the left one, and approached slowly.

Clyde looked at him coldly. “Where the hell have you been? And where’s Clennon?”

Hawken shrugged and said bitterly, “The son-of-a-bitch! He untied me and wanted me to help him get away from you. I said all right and we took off. We hadn’t gone ten miles before he pulled his gun on me. Said he didn’t trust me and was goin’ on alone. I tried to talk him out of it, but he threatened to shoot me if I didn’t git.”

Lacy said nervously, “Clyde, he’s lying.”

“Probably. Get off your horse, Hawken.”

Hawken dismounted meekly. Clyde swung down, the gun in his hand. He rammed it in Hawken’s back with one hand, while with his other he carefully searched him. When he had finished he went to Hawken’s horse and searched the saddlebags. He looked puzzled as he holstered his gun and turned away. He glanced up at Lacy and said, “He hasn’t got it. Maybe it’s the truth.”

Lacy didn’t answer. Her eyes on Hawken made him faintly uncomfortable. It was as though she were looking into his thoughts.

Clyde said, “All right. Mount up. But from here on you pull your own weight.”

Hawken nodded agreeably. “Sure. But since when haven’t I pulled my own weight?”

He mounted and rode away to push some stragglers into the bunch. At a safe distance, he permitted himself a small grin of satisfaction.

He had things going his way now. Clyde would relax his vigilance, believing Hawken to be unarmed. He could recover the revolver from beside the dead cottonwood when they passed, and hide it in his boot.

He began to plan ahead. Once Clyde was out of the way, the rest would be easy. There were plenty of men in Utah who would buy the herd, even with the brands unchanged if he didn't want to take the time for that. What difference would it make if he had to sell them at a reduced price? He'd still have more money than he'd ever hoped to have.

And Lacy was a pretty thing. Once Clyde and Rufe were out of the way, she'd come around. Women were all alike. Give them a smell of money and their principles went out the window. Lacy would be no different.

He began to feel good. He had an excellent plan and a better than excellent chance of carrying it off. There'd be no more of drifting from town to town for him, no more of risking imprisonment or death just to get a few dollars. He'd buy a saloon somewhere. That was a real life for a man. All you did was stand behind the bar and watch the money roll in.

The hours passed, and at last Hawken saw the familiar cottonwood log off to his right at the edge of the valley.

He swung toward it casually, ostensibly to

push straggling cattle back into the herd. He dismounted at the exact spot he had left the gun and stopped, snatching it up from the grass and stuffing it into his right boot. Then, aware that Clyde or Lacy might be watching, he lifted his horse's right front hoof and examined it. Straightening, he mounted and continued on his way.

He doubted if Clyde would suspect his stopping beside that log. After all, it was only good sense to inspect a hoof you thought might be about to cause a horse to go lame. All the horses had traveled farther on a single set of shoes than they should.

From the corner of his eye, he saw Clyde turn and swing toward him. He felt tension begin to rise in his chest. He didn't want a showdown now. Lacy was still over there across the valley and she had a rifle. Hawken didn't want to shoot it out with her.

Clyde rode up and asked suspiciously, "What the hell was that all about?"

"What was what all about?" Hawken asked innocently.

"Getting down behind that dead tree."

Hawken managed to look surprised. "Just looking at my horse's hoof. I thought he was favoring it. Figured he might have a rock in the frog."

"Did he?"

Hawken shook his head. “Maybe it was a stone bruise from all that rough country I covered last night and this morning.” He rode the horse around Clyde in a circle. “See how he favors that right front foot?”

Clyde scowled. “No I don’t. He looks all right to me.” He studied Hawken for a few moments suspiciously. Then he rode back to rejoin Lacy and Rufe.

CHAPTER 18

AT SUNDOWN, Clyde called a halt. Lacy dismounted dispiritedly, and Clyde helped Rufe from his saddle. Rufe was listless, seeming to have no interest in anything, but his mind was lucid again, at least, and he knew where he was.

Clyde caught himself studying Lacy. She puzzled him. She seemed almost as listless as Rufe, as though she no longer cared what happened. Their success so far made no visible impression on her spirits. Perhaps she was thinking of Carrie, thinking that now Clyde would go to her. Perhaps she thought the love they had experienced back in the reservation was but a passing thing of loneliness and need, a thing without permanency.

A feeling of guilt assailed Clyde. He knew that he had to hurt either Lacy or Carrie. He also knew which of them it had to be.

Somewhat irritably, he stared out into the valley at the sleek, fat herd of cattle. He realized suddenly that they gave him no more satisfaction than they did Lacy.

The herd had solved nothing, really; he knew

that now. But as he stared at the cattle, his mouth firmed out stubbornly. He'd gone through hell to get them. He'd come this far and now he'd go on with it to the bitter end. Carrie would have her money. Johnny's life would not have been spent in vain. And Clyde himself might know release from his obligation to Carrie—someday even release from his love for her. For he knew now that it never would have worked. He knew what Lacy had meant when she'd asked what kind of woman could send the ones she loved into mortal danger for money. Lacy had meant that money and position and security were more important to Carrie than people were.

He kicked a dead cedar branch savagely. Then he began to gather wood for a fire.

He built a big fire out of pure perversity, realizing that he didn't care if it was seen, by Indians or anyone else that happened to be around.

Lacy watched him, an unreadable expression in her eyes. The curve of her mouth was sad and dispirited, he thought. Whenever he met her glance, she looked away.

His anger grew. For a while he tried fighting it down, but at last he let it have its way. He looked stonily at Lacy. "Well, what's the matter? We're safely out of the reservation. We can rest a few days and let Rufe recover. We've got what we came after."

"Yes, Clyde."

He kicked the dirt in exasperation. "Something's eating you. What is it?"

"Nothing Clyde."

He said angrily, "I wasn't lying to you back there in the reservation. We're free, Lacy. Doesn't that mean anything to you?"

"Are we free, Clyde?"

He turned away furiously, "Oh hell!"

He added more wood to the fire. The thing that was eating him kept gnawing away. He swung to face her again. "Is Hawken worryin' you? If he is, you can quit. He's unarmed and I intend to see that he stays that way."

Lacy didn't answer.

He sat down beside her and took her hand. Anger drained out of him, leaving gentleness in its wake. "Lacy, what is it?"

Her eyes were bright with unshed tears. "I'm sorry, Clyde. I just can't help it."

"Can't help what?"

"Wondering what you and I can build together on a foundation of theft and killing."

He pulled her to him and kissed her mouth. It was cool and yielding. Her arms went around him with almost frantic strength. "Clyde, can't you see? To sell these cattle, you're going to have to deal with thieves. It will snowball like lies, Clyde. To cover up this crime you'll have to commit another. And another. There'll be no end to it."

His anger returned and he pulled away. “Are you trying to tell me you’ve changed your mind? Are you trying to say you don’t want to go with me?”

A tear ran from her brimming eyes and across her smooth cheek. “No Clyde. I’ll go with you, whatever you decide.”

“That’s good of you,” he said sarcastically. He got up and stamped away to picket the horses out for the night.

Hawken was cutting meat from the calf carcass that had been on Clyde’s saddle. He didn’t look up, though Valle stared at him hard and truculently.

He picketed the horses, then wandered out into the valley and sat down on a rock. He stared at the grazing cattle moodily in the gray dusk light.

What was the matter with him? What was the matter with Lacy? They ought to be jubilant and glad it was over. They’d settled what was between them that night out under the stars. Why couldn’t they go on from there?

Clyde knew the answer to that, however he hated to admit that he did. Lacy had never approved the theft of the cattle and she could hardly be expected to approve it now. Yet, approving or not, she was willing to go with him.

What more did he want? He searched himself sourly, wondering.

He did want more. He wanted Lacy’s approval

and support. It was as simple as that. He wanted Lacy's approval more than anything else in the world.

He got up and returned to camp. Hawken was cooking meat over the fire. Lacy sat as he had left her. Rufe was lying down.

Clyde went over and sat down beside Rufe. "How do you feel, Rufe?"

"Weak, Clyde. Drained out." Rufe grinned faintly. "But we done it, didn't we. We done it. Carrie's sure goin' to be proud of us."

"Yeah. I reckon she will."

"You an' her goin' to get married now, Clyde?"

Clyde frowned without answering. Rufe asked, "How many cattle we got, Clyde?"

"Almost a thousand."

Rufe chuckled. "Boy, I'd like to hear Carrie when we tell her. We sure made them damn Yankees pay, didn't we?"

Clyde felt like saying, "We paid too, Rufe." But he didn't. Rufe was elated and happy. Let him stay that way.

Getting up, he was thinking that everything in life had its price. The price of this herd had been Johnny's life, Rufe's wound, and Clyde's integrity. The price had been paid, but had it all been paid? Might there not be, as Lacy said, an even greater price to be paid in the years ahead?

Lacy took meat and water to Rufe, who ate

hungrily tonight for the first time. Clyde wasn't particularly hungry. Just tired and discouraged. But he ate anyway, knowing he needed it.

Hawken made him uneasy. There was an ugly smugness about the man that puzzled him. It was as though Hawken knew something Valle didn't. It was as though Hawken, instead of Clyde himself, had the upper hand.

Clyde studied Hawken, hating him bitterly. Hawken's face, the part of it visible above his beard, was grimy with sweat and dirty. His eyes, too close together, were mocking and cold and held a touch of triumph.

Triumph over what? Clyde glanced at Lacy. Her rifle lay close beside her. She hadn't moved all evening without the rifle.

His own rifle was in his hand. His revolver was in its holster.

He stared at Hawken again, and a new, disturbing thought occurred to him. What if Hawken had overpowered and murdered Clennon? What if he had lied when he said Clennon had gone on without him?

He remembered the old cottonwood log beside which Hawken had examined his horse's hoof. Suddenly a chill ran along his spine. If Hawken had killed Clennon, it followed that he now had Clennon's gun. He could have ridden ahead and hidden it beside the dead cottonwood log. He could have recovered it when he stopped to examine his horse's hoof. He could have it now.

Hawken, disturbed by the intensity of Clyde's stare, looked up and met his eyes. And Clyde knew the time had come.

CHAPTER 19

ODDLY, he was not afraid. Instead, he welcomed the final showdown. But it didn't come. He stared at Hawken and the man stared back. Nothing happened.

Could he have been wrong? He doubted it. Hawken had the gun all right, but he didn't intend to use it until the time was right, until he was sure of coming out on top.

The thing to do was to alert Lacy and then move in on Hawken. Take him by surprise. Search him.

But what if he'd hidden the gun? He'd be warned. He'd know that Valle knew he had it. No. The best way was to go on as though he had no suspicions of the man. Alert Lacy and then watch and wait.

Clyde got up, slowly and casually. He turned his back deliberately on Hawken and walked toward Lacy.

Rufe had his head on a saddle and was staring at the dancing flames of the fire. Suddenly he sat bolt upright. He yelled in a cracked voice, "Clyde! Look out!"

Clyde whirled, his rifle leveled. Hawken's gun blasted.

A blow like the kick of a horse struck Clyde in the thigh. His leg went out from under him. His rifle fired, its muzzle pointed at the sky.

Panic ran through him like a grass fire. He'd bungled it! And now Hawken would kill him.

Rolling, he snatched at his revolver. His right leg was numb. Lacy screamed.

Hawken fired again, his gun pointing, not at Clyde, but at something behind him.

Clyde leveled his revolver and thumbed back the hammer. Hawken swung his gun muzzle toward Clyde.

In the instant before he fired, Clyde saw panic come to Hawken's eyes and instead of firing, Hawken flung himself sideways to hit the ground rolling. Clyde's shot missed.

Hawken scrambled to hands and knees and lunged for the darkness beyond the circle of firelight. Clyde fired again, but missed again because of the way Hawken was weaving back and forth. And then the man was gone.

Clyde swung his head, a colder fear in his heart than any he had ever felt before. Hawken had fired at Lacy. Oh God . . .

Lacy was on the ground, on her hands and knees beside the still body of Rufe Thebus.

Valle tried to get up, but his leg wouldn't support him. He crawled toward Lacy, aware of

Hawken's presence out there in the darkness, aware of Lacy's danger.

Her eyes were filled with shock, her face gray with it. Her head had been against Rufe's chest, but now she was rising.

Clyde struck her shoulder with the flat of his hand and flung her away. She lost her balance and fell. He said sharply, "Move! For God's sake get out of the light!"

Hawken might be momentarily demoralized by his narrow escape, but out in the safety of the darkness, he wouldn't stay that way long. He'd be coming back. And when he did . . .

Lacy scrambled away from him and he followed, clumsily dragging his numbed leg behind. He'd lost the rifle when Hawken's bullet knocked him down. It lay behind him now, gleaming dully in the light of the fire.

Lacy's rifle, too, lay back there in the firelight beside Rufe's body.

She halted, and swung around, running back. He yelled, "Damn it, don't come back. Get out of the light. I'm coming."

Her face was stricken, but she turned and ran until she was safely hidden in the darkness. He reached her a few moments later and she fell to her knees beside him. "Clyde, you're hurt!"

"In the leg." His pants were soaked with blood. He fumbled in his pocket until he found a knife. He cut his pants away from the wound. Lacy stripped off her shirt and mopped at it carefully. "We've got to have some light."

"Light be damned," he grunted. "If we strike a match, we're dead. Is it bleeding slow or in spurts?"

He could feel her hands on his thigh. She cried, "Clyde, I can't tell for sure. But I think it's a steady bleeding."

"All right. Does the hole go clear through? Do you feel any bone splinters?"

He knew she was almost hysterical, but she replied with a shocked steadiness, "There's a small hole in the front and a ragged one in back. I can't feel any bone splinters, but it's so slick . . ."

Clyde said, "All right, Lacy. Tie your shirt around it. I've got to get Hawken before he gets us."

Her hands were trembling violently as she tied the shirt around his leg. He waited impatiently for her to finish.

In his mind he was counting up the shots he had fired. He thought he had fired twice, or three times. That left him with two shots at least, possibly three.

How about Hawken? He had fired twice too. But had his gun been fully loaded? Clennon had quite possibly fired the gun at game before Hawken got it. And Hawken might have killed Clennon with it.

He shrugged, knowing he had to assume

Hawken's gun was loaded, for it was possible that Clennon had been carrying spare cartridges.

He put his mouth close to Lacy's ear. "Stay here. Don't make a sound and above all don't move. Do you understand?"

She nodded her head. Her body was trembling violently as though she had a chill. Valle gripped her arm in reassurance.

His leg wasn't broken. Apparently the bone was untouched. So there was no damn reason in the world why he couldn't stand. He *had* to stand. He'd never catch Hawken crawling on the ground like an animal.

He came to a sitting position. Doubling his left leg, he put his entire weight on it, forcing himself up with his hands.

Pain shot wildly through his right leg as he bent it. He felt sweat pop out on his face. Gritting his teeth, he came erect.

Pain came in dizzying waves and his head reeled. He swayed and almost fell, but he put his mind and will to staying upright, and gradually the dizziness passed.

He took a hesitant step and discovered that the leg would support him if he favored it.

Now, he stopped. He made his ragged breathing slow, and listened intently. He heard nothing, but he didn't move. He stood thus, utterly still, listening, for a full five minutes.

And at last he was rewarded. Over across the

clearing which contained the fire, he heard a twig snap.

Instantly, he swung around, his gun ready. There could be no wild, hasty, hopeful shots tonight. He could depend on having only two shots in the gun. He had to make each one count.

Carefully, slowly, he bent his knees and crouched. The pain in his right leg was now almost intolerable. He felt around on the ground, praying his hand would encounter a rock. It did. He picked up the rock and came erect again.

Again he waited for dizziness to pass. Then, aiming carefully, he flung the rock across the clearing to the right of the place he had heard the noise. And froze, listening.

The rock clattered in the brush, in the dry, dead leaves that still clung to it. Clyde waited for the roar of Hawken's shot, but it didn't come. Instead, he heard a dry, metallic click.

It took him an instant to puzzle it out. Then a grim smile touched his mouth. Hawken had fired all right, but his gun was empty. The click had been the hammer falling.

Then Hawken had to try for one of the rifles lying out beside the fire.

Grinning fiercely, Clyde hobbled carefully toward the fire. He had to be close, but not close enough so that the fire illuminated him.

He stopped, his grin fading. Hawken was unhurt. He could afford to wait until the fire died. But Clyde couldn't afford to wait. His leg was bleeding steadily. Weakness and shock were gradually overcoming him. By the time the fire died, he'd be on the ground, unconscious.

How to make Hawken try for the rifle now? Clyde's brain worked at the problem feverishly. And then his grin returned. If Hawken thought they were getting away . . .

He turned carefully and retraced his steps to where Lacy lay. He whispered, "Lacy."

"Yes Clyde?"

He said, "Slip away as quietly as you can. Go to the horses and get there without making a sound if you can. Take all the time you want. When you get there, release one of them and quirt him good on the rump. Make him run away. Then move off to one side and lie down. Wait for me there and don't make a sound."

"Why . . ."

"Don't argue, honey. It's the only way."

"All right, Clyde." She made a soft rustling as she got up. Then she was gone. He listened intently, but heard no sound.

He turned and moved back toward the clearing until he could see it clearly. His head was becoming lighter. He knew he had not much time.

If Hawken's gun was empty, he'd have to try for one of the rifles when he heard the horse and thought Clyde and Lacy were getting away. When he did . . .

Clyde waited. His lightheadedness increased. He wished he had a tree to lean against, but he didn't. He didn't even have a stick to use as a cane.

His leg was warm and wet with blood all the way to his boot.

Suddenly, he heard the sharp crack of a quirt, and afterward the thunderous crashing of a horse stampeding away toward the river. His muscles tensed. Would Hawken go for the ruse?

The sounds of the horse slowly died away. Clyde, listening, heard a crash across the clearing.

He saw a blurred shape run out of the darkness beyond the fire and approach it. Hawken came into the light at a shambling run, and Clyde raised his gun.

But he couldn't fire without giving Hawken a chance. In spite of all the man had done, Clyde couldn't shoot him like a clay duck in a shooting gallery.

Inwardly, he cursed himself for a fool. But even as he did, he called out, "Hawken! Freeze!"

Hawken dived for the rifle. Rolling, clutching the rifle, he swung the muzzle toward Clyde.

Clyde fired instinctively. He saw the dust his bullet kicked up, and knew his shot had missed.

One more. Only one. Hawken came bounding clumsily to his feet like a bear. By the way he swung the rifle, by the way he sighted along its barrel, Clyde knew the man could see him, however dimly, by the dying fire's light.

Deliberately he raised his Colt's. Deliberately he brought it to bear on Hawken's chest. And fired.

Hawken's rifle discharged immediately afterward, its roar blending with that of Clyde's revolver. Then it slipped from his hands and clattered to the ground.

He stood for a moment, hunched a little. Then his knees buckled. He fell forward slowly and lay still in the dust.

Clyde started to run. His leg went out from under him. He fell not a yard from where Rufe lay. With a wary glance toward Hawken, he crawled to Rufe and grabbed his wrist. But Rufe was dead.

Running feet approached him through the brush. Light feet. Lacy's feet. Then she was down on the ground beside him, weeping without restraint. "Are you all right? Clyde, Clyde, are you all right?"

He nodded. She helped him rise and walked beside him to the fire, supporting him, steadying him. Then she went running to her saddle for the bundle she kept behind it and her only dress . . .

The sun beat warmly upon them as they rose from their task of covering the graves they had dug for Rufe and for Hawken.

Lacy's face was dirty, her hair a mop of tangled silk. There was mud on her hands.

Her eyes held his as she waited for him to say what they would do.

He looked out across the valley at the cattle, widely scattered now. He said, "Come on, Lacy."

They mounted. Trailing Rufe's and Hawken's horses, they rode into the valley and began to gather up the herd.

They drove all day, and at nightfall came out of the river canyon and reached a vast, wide, broken plain. Here, where a road from the north met the river trail, Clyde saw two people waiting. They had a map set up, and apparently had been here several days.

Carrie looked different than she had back home. Dressed in men's clothes, she looked smaller, more helpless than she ever had before.

He let the herd scatter and dismounted uncertainly beside her. She flung herself into his arms. "Clyde! You did it! I knew you would!"

He glanced at her male companion, missing neither the man's jealous anger nor the sudden, naked greed in his eyes, as he looked away toward the herd.

Clyde said, "If you knew I'd do it, why did you come?"

"To help, Clyde. Only to help."

"Who's your friend?"

"Wayne Dawson. Clyde, I couldn't come all

that way alone." Her flushed face betrayed her. She could not meet his eyes.

Suddenly, for the first time, Clyde saw all the way to Carrie's core. Carrie had not asked about Johnny, or Rufe; she had eyes only for the thousand cattle spread out on the wide plain.

Obviously she had not trusted Clyde and the others or she would not have felt it necessary to come.

Clyde said, "Aren't you going to ask where Johnny and Rufe are?"

He could see that she was now thinking of them for the first time. "Where are they, Clyde?"

"They're dead," he said brutally. "They're part of the price tag on that herd of cattle."

She flinched at his cruelty, but there were no tears in her for Johnny and Rufe. Nor, Clyde realized suddenly, would there have been tears in her for Lacy or himself.

He said, watching Lacy approaching reluctantly from the herd, "They're yours, Carrie. Yours and Dawson's. You and he can take it from here."

"No, Clyde. No. I want . . ."

He smiled faintly. "What do you want, Carrie? Do you really know?"

"Clyde, you're worn out. You're not thinking straight. Get some sleep and then we'll talk."

He looked down at her, realizing at last that he had spent his life loving something that simply didn't exist. He had loved a woman that was only a shell, a glittering facade. Lacy had been right. All the things Carrie had done, the things he had worshipped her for doing, had been done for herself. Her motives had been neither compassion nor love. She had only tried to cling to the past by keeping those that were part of it close to her.

She needed none of them now. She had the substance of the past, the money, the security, in her grasp.

Clyde said, "Good bye, Carrie. I hope Dawson's right for you. And I hope, now, that you can forget the war."

Her eyes sparkled dangerously. Lacy rode up and sat her horse looking down at Carrie. Lacy's face was soft with pity.

Carrie's mouth twisted and her face turned white. She said with harsh anger, "You did this! My own sister! You turned him against me. How did you do it, by sharing his bed? You . . ."

Clyde looked at Lacy. She was painfully flushed, and her eyes were stricken. He said, "Come on, Lacy."

He rode away, with Carrie's vindictive voice harsh in his ears. Lacy followed silently.

He didn't stop until the herd and the camp were out of sight.

He said, "This will do for now. Get down, Lacy."

She dismounted timidly, and his arms closed

hard around her. He said, “Lacy, we’re free, and the whole world’s ours. But someday when the Indians have been pushed out of the White River Valley, I’d like to go back. I’d like for us to settle there.”

He thought her smiling mouth and sparkling eyes were the most beautiful things he had ever seen. She raised her face and he kissed her, hard and long, as though he would never get enough, as though he would never let her go.

MADE IN THE USA

Books are produced in the United States using U.S.-based materials

Books are printed using a revolutionary new process called THINKtech™ that lowers energy usage by 70% and increases overall quality

Books are durable and flexible because of Smyth-sewing

Paper is sourced using environmentally responsible foresting methods and the paper is acid-free

Center Point Large Print
600 Brooks Road / PO Box 1
Thorndike, ME 04986-0001 USA

(207) 568-3717

US & Canada:
1 800 929-9108
www.centerpointlargeprint.com